I0586808

Sign up for book announcements and special deals at:

AWBALDWIN.COM

ACCLAIM FOR THE

RELIC SERIES NOVELS

BY AWARD WINNING AUTHOR
A.W. BALDWIN

DESERT GUARDIAN

A moonshining hermit.
A campus bookworm.
A midnight murder.

Can an unlikely duo and a whitewater crew save themselves and an ancient Aztec battlefield from deadly looters?

Ethan's world turns upside-down when he slips off the edge of red-rock cliffs into a world of twisting ravines and coveted artifacts. Saved by a mysterious desert recluse named Relic, Ethan must join a whitewater rafting group and make his way back to civilization. But someone in the gorge is killing to protect their illegal dig for ancient treasures... When Anya, the lead whitewater guide, is attacked, he must divert the killer into the dark canyon night, but his most deadly pursuer is not who he thinks... Ethan struggles to save his new friends, face his own mortality, and unravel the chilling murders. But when they flee the secluded canyon, a lethal hunter is hot on their trail...

RAPTOR CANYON

A moonshining hermit.
A big city lawyer.
A $35 million con job.

What if you discover you've helped your boss hide a murder and defile a pristine canyon? Can a young lawyer and moonshining hermit save rare petroglyphs and monkey-wrench a corrupt land deal in the Utah canyons?

An impromptu murder leads a hermit named Relic to an unlikely set of dinosaur petroglyphs and swindlers using the unique rock art to turn the canyon into a high-end tourist trap. When attorney, Wyatt, and his boss travel to the site to approve the next phase of financing, Wyatt learns the truth about their unorthodox role in the project. A corrupt security chief runs Relic and Wyatt off of the site and the unusual pair must endure each other while fleeing though white-water rapids, remote gorges, and hidden caverns. Faye, who shares covert ties with the treasured site, catalyzes their desperate plan to fight back and to recast the fate of Raptor Canyon.

"Raptor Canyon is a ton of fun… the playful dialogue between Wyatt and Relic was a pleasure to read… Highly recommended!"

– Landon Beach, Bestselling author of *The Sail*, Grand Master Adventure Writers' Finalist Award

Five Star Rating from Readers' Favorite:

"A hoot of an adventure novel… most highly recommended."

Onlinebookclub.org four out of four Star Review:

"…captivating, with hair raising experiences that will have your muscles tensed up and your heart pounding… I enthusiastically recommend it to anyone who enjoys mesmerizing, fast-paced novels."

WINGS OVER GHOST CREEK

A moonshining hermit.
A reluctant pilot.
A $5 million plunder.

What if your archeology field class was hiding assassins and dealers in black-market treasure?

Owen discovers a murdered corpse at a college-run archeological dig in the Utah outback but when he and a park service pilot try to reach the sheriff for help, their plane is shot from the sky. Owen must ditch the aircraft in the Colorado River, where he is saved by a moonshining hermit named Relic. The two flee from the sniper and circle back to warn the students. They must trek through rugged canyon country, unravel a baffling mystery, and foil a remarkable form of thievery. Suzy, a student at the dig, helps spearhead their escape but the unique team of crooks has a surprise for them...

Grand Master Adventure Writers' Finalist Award 2020

"Another gripping Relic tale with trademark wit and deft expression"

> – Jacob P. Avila, Cave Diver, Grand Master Adventure Writers' Award Winner

"[A] humorous, fun, and well-plotted adventure,"

> – Landon Beach, Bestselling author of The Sail, Grand Master Adventure Writers' Finalist Award

Onlinebookclub.org Review:

> Wings offers "…action-packed adventure and nerve-racking suspense, with a touch of romance and humor mixed in"

> Baldwin has a "gift for capturing the reader's attention at the beginning and keeping them spellbound"

> Wings has "lots of thrilling action and twists"

DIAMONDS OF DEVIL'S TAIL

A moonshining hermit.
An English major.
A $4 million jewel heist.

When diamonds appear in a remote canyon stream, whitewater rafters and artifact thieves set off in a deadly race to the source.

Brayden, an aspiring writer, works in a Chicago insurance firm with his ambitious uncle when they embark on a wilderness whitewater adventure. On a remote hike, they find their colleague, Dylan, dead in the sand, a handful of gems in his fist. When thieves charge in, Brayden flees deeper into the canyon, where he encounters a gin-brewing recluse named Relic. Brayden's uncle is cornered and cuts a deal with the thieves, but they each have a surprise for the other... and the rafters have ideas of their own about getting rich quick... Brayden and Relic must become allies, traverse the harsh desert, and beat the thieves to the hidden gems. Brayden must confront his uncle about suspicious payments at their insurance firm and what he was really doing at the stream where Dylan was killed…

Can they discover the truth, find the lost jewels, and protect the rafters from grenade-tossing thieves?

A.W. BALDWIN
DESERT GUARDIAN

Copyright 2016 by A.W. Baldwin
Copyright Second Edition 2017 by A.W. Baldwin
Copyright Third Edition 2020 by A.W. Baldwin

ISBN   978-0-99969134-0-4 Hardbound
ISBN   978-0-9996913-1-1 Paperback
ISBN   978-0-9996913-4-2 eBook

Cover art by Daniel Thiede.
Map and chapter heading art by Nate Baldwin.

For Mom and Dad

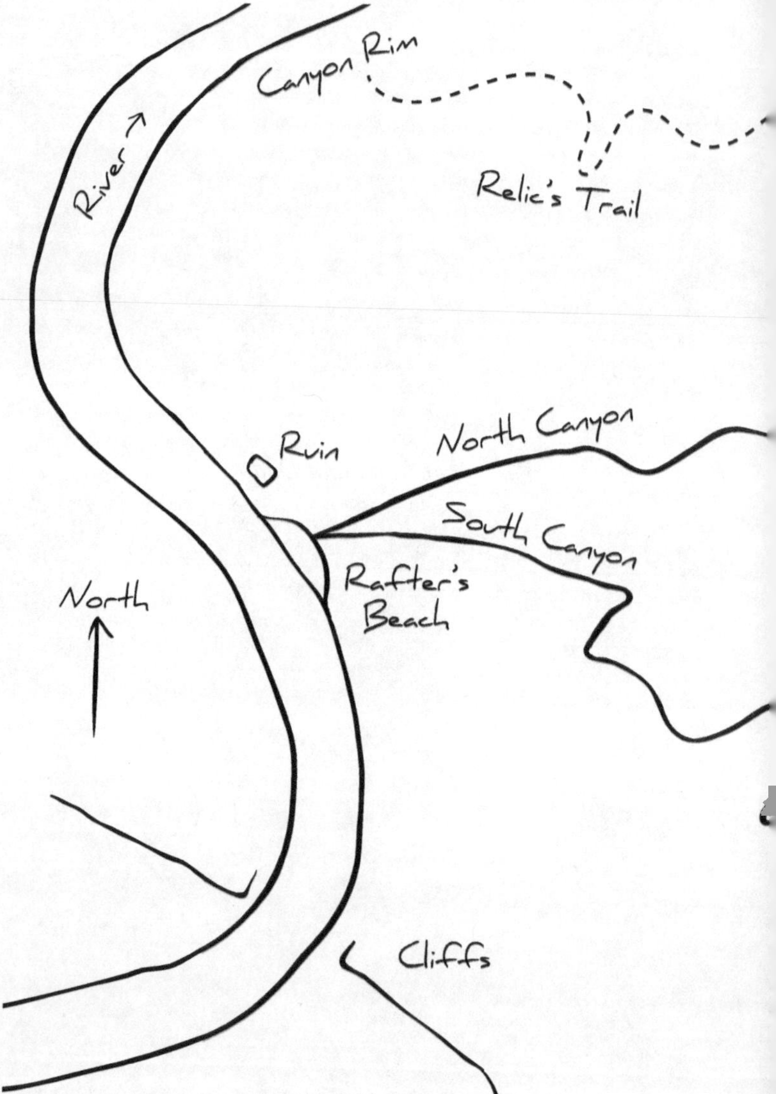

Canyon Rim

River →

Relic's Trail

Ruin

North Canyon

South Canyon

Rafter's
Beach

North

Cliffs

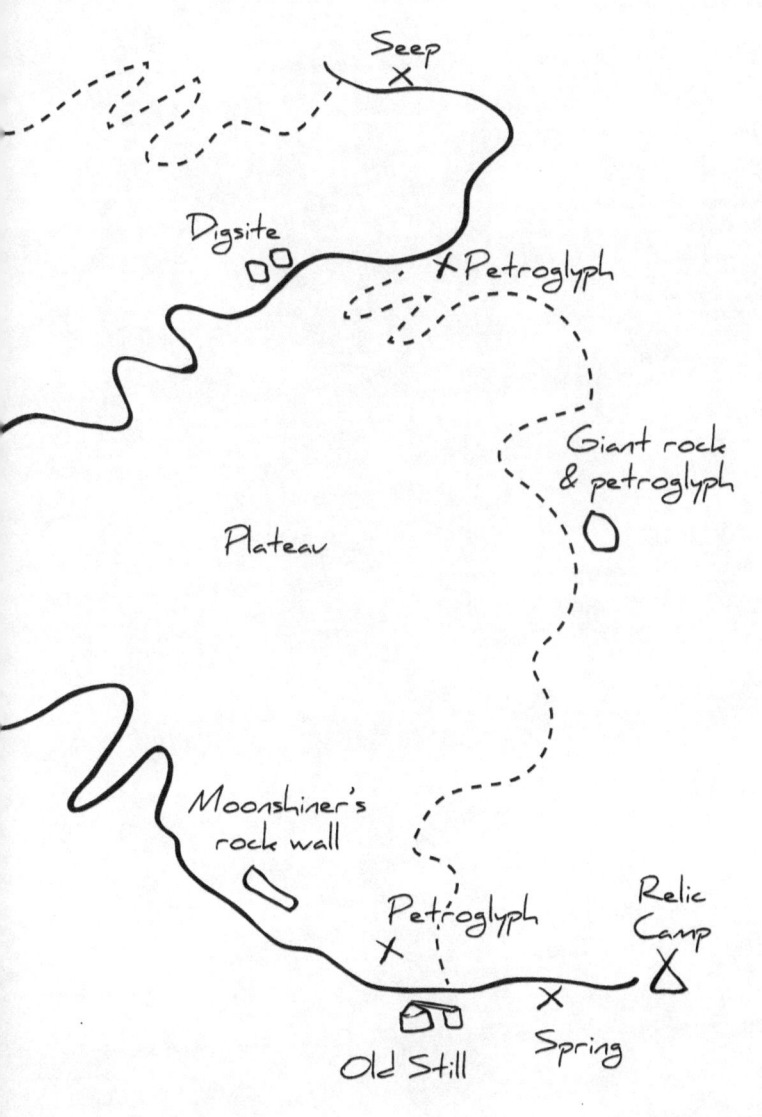

Seep
X

Digsite
☐☐

X Petroglyph

Giant rock
& petroglyph
◯

Plateau

Moonshiner's
rock wall
▭

Petroglyph
X

Relic
Camp
△

Old Still
◖◗

X
Spring

PROLOGUE

1224 A.D.

Voices boomed like spring thunder as eight Mexica war-
riors trotted around the canyon bend in loose formation,
grunting in rhythm. Woolen cloths of ochre and tan held
rows of parrot feathers upright on their heads. Circles of
pounded gold at their temples kept their chinstraps in
place but their necklaces bounced and shimmered like
light on a roiling wave.

A smothering fear squeezed the young breath out
of Ahote. He and the other pueblo men hid, ready to
ambush from both sides of the arroyo. They knew the
lives of their families depended on what they did next.

The lead warrior wore a leather breastplate painted with the head of a smoke-breathing monster with al-
mond-eyes and canine teeth. His armor was gashed and
worn along the edges, the wear of a long campaign. They
carried knives of flint or chert and hung short bows and
arrows in quivers over their shoulders. Their marching
song echoed eerily up the narrow canyon, drowning everything in its approach. They were only four hundred
feet away and closing fast.

The Mexica had been raiding the homes of Ahote's people for years, forcing the pueblo families to build higher and more remote fortifications. The enemy came not for food or territory, though they took that, too, when it pleased them. But they came mostly for slaves. Ahote had heard tales in the darkest nights, when voices were hoarse and campfires flashed hellish shadows on the human face. His people were worked to death in quarries or forced to clean canals of human waste in a giant, floating city many days travel to the south. Worse yet, some of their people had been sacrificed to the gods of the Mexica, their hearts torn from their chests. Ahote's mother and three sisters were, at that moment, scrambling up the narrow cracks and ledges above the box canyon to escape. Lenmana, his oldest sister, had her infant strapped to her back.

He tried again to breathe.

The Mexica were only twenty feet away, their fearsome song expelling all other sounds from the canyon. Ahote's heart pumped until even his fingers throbbed.

Cheveyo, the pueblo leader, let loose a piercing cry that stopped the Mexica chant, suspending time in a moment that would be history.

The invaders' spell was broken. Cheveyo fired an arrow deep into the Mexica leader's throat. The other pueblo men shot arrows from both sides of the narrow canyon and three enemies fell still in the dirt. Five others drew weapons but struggled with arrows in their legs or shoulders. They tried to form a circle, but the pueblo men swarmed over them with short, chert-tipped spears and clubs.

Two pueblo men and all of the Mexica died in a fury that lasted only minutes.

The pueblo leader told six men to take their dead to be buried honorably under a high ledge above the arroyo. He told the rest to hide the dead Mexica to delay pursuit. The rest of Ahote's people, twenty-two in all, had fled ahead of the pueblo fighters, up the narrow trail that followed the spring creek deep into the side canyon. It led to a place with no exit, save one - a tiny wedge through which a person could climb to a mid-level ridge. At a switchback on that ridge, it was possible to scramble over a large boulder and onto a shelf above. If you knew the way, you could then go higher, and eventually out onto the high plain above the canyons where no Mexica would follow.

Ahote helped drag the Mexica bodies to a spot behind a large chunk of sandstone. It was the first time he'd seen men die at the hands of other men and the first time he'd touched the dead of another tribe. He held one by the arm and pulled it over rough ground. The body snagged, then jostled past a rock, seeming to stir on its own volition. He leapt back-ward, spooked for a moment that the warrior had come back from the dead to grab him.

In the wet season, when water surged down the canyon, it pooled in a gooseneck fifty yards long and deposited sand that was easy to dig. The men sweated heavily under the noon sun, for the makeshift grave had to be deep enough for eight bodies. They took a few knives from the dead but left the strange headgear, necklaces, and metal-studded chin straps. Ahote took a pair of leather sandals. To hide the graves, the pueblo men swept the top of the sand with their feet and tufts of grass. This group of Mexica was an advance troop sent to scout the side canyon. More could be coming at any moment.

CHAPTER 1

Ethan pedaled harder, his front tire spinning, a blur of spokes and space propelling him over the slick-rock trail. He'd come to the canyon country to celebrate his sociology degree, down a few beers, and sweat out the murk and mold from busboy jobs, grim schedules, and a pair of particularly erratic professors. His wheels hummed evenly beneath him, mesmerizing him, unreeling his thoughts…

Her sudden death in a car accident last semester had shaken him. It wasn't as if they were going to get married or something. In fact, they'd only been dating a few weeks when they entered a mutual hiatus of sorts, seeing other people, doing other things, leaving their experience to simmer in the background for a while. Probably wouldn't have gone anywhere. After all, they'd made a joint decision to stop dating each other and see what happened. Still, he sometimes saw her soft eyes in his dreams.

He crested a rise, his heart and legs pumping in rhythm, and angled off the path across an open expanse of sandstone. He coasted toward a grand horizon of earthen haze and backlit sky, standing on his pedals, letting gravity speed him along the curving rock. Her eyes seemed to share his view across the expanse and then, in a blink, fell closed.

Suddenly, the slick-rock disappeared beneath him and for a moment he hung weightless, past the solid ground, past the precipice, past his beating heart, past all hope of going back. He gripped the handlebar tightly but he could not breathe, shift his gaze, or even turn his head. Time and motion became entangled and suspended together in one graceful, dreadful second.

Then hell itself swallowed him down, past the red rock cliffs, through a gullet of cracked stone and hardened crust toward a talus slope of sand and concrete-colored scree. His bike slipped from his feet and soared ahead of him, held by fingers he could see, and knew were his, but could not will to move. In a flash, he was below another line of cliffs and the slope below was close upon him.

He had no time to watch the bike spin from his grip or to brace his legs. His feet struck first, skidding for a second, then pirouetting in a full backward summersault, slamming the ground again then falling onto his back, rolling sideways, over and over, his arms flailing and striking gravel, skidding between rocks the size of helmets.

He slid across a pocket of sand and slowed until he reached a small ledge and finally stopped. His skin felt torched, his head aching like a cheap whiskey hangover. His stomach clenched at the smell of blood and dust, his nose and mouth like they'd been scoured raw by sandpaper. Shades of rust and rose blurred into an unknown distance. He hung there, one leg over the edge, and in the time it took for a single breath, it all dimmed into shadows.

CHAPTER 2

Relic pulled the back of his graying hair through a rubber band and kicked fine dirt across exhausted lumps of charcoal under the still. He wiped a sweaty hand across his tangled buffalo-beard. His dark eyes followed the gentle curve of copper tubing that ran above the drum, then down toward the stone floor. He let one more drop of condensation fall into a crockery jug and jammed a cork in the top.

He sat on his bench beneath the sandstone overhang and took a quick inventory. Twenty jugs of homemade gin lined the back wall, half buried in sand in the cool shade of the shallow cave. Not bad for this early in the season, he thought. Plenty to sell, plenty to drink. There sat the sum total of his wealth, his own personal savings and investment plan, safe and sound in the remote desert of Canyonlands.

Relic reached for his daypack and pulled it toward him. New, it had been a deep evergreen color. Now worn and patched, the Utah dust had turned it a mottled sage. He'd left his Colt revolver in the main camp to the south. The sling-shot was all he really needed for the occasional pygmy rattlesnake.

He rose, a bit more stiffly than in younger years, and walked outside the cave and downslope to a small spring seeping from an outcrop. Long blades of grass and a vivid fern suckled on the damp earth around the spring, a miniature oasis amid the heated rock. He mumbled thanks to the spring, as he usually did, then put his whole face into the small pool and sucked the water in until his stomach could hold no more. He stood and wiped the moisture from his face. A man had to drink a gallon a day to stay alive in this stunning desert.

To the north, a puff of dust rose from the steep slopes. His eyes scanned the ground for the mountain sheep that came there sometimes, but a flash of metal told him it was something foreign and troublesome. A harsh clatter echoed against the rock walls and he moved farther into the open, his eyes searching higher up the small canyon.

"Well, shit on a shingle." A high plume of dust floated toward him from above, elongated by the breeze.

He heard the sound of something thudding into the dirt, something softer than what he'd heard before. For a better view, he stepped higher up and around a car-sized boulder.

"Gawdammit," he swore to himself. The commotion had to be man-made.

He pulled compact binoculars from his pocket and scanned the scene. Was that a dead branch hanging from the ledge or a man's leg?

"Christ, some poor bugger just died up there." He lowered the binoculars and looked above and all around the area. Nothing moved, and the air grew quiet. Who was it? How did he get there? Did he die in the fall? Where the hell did he come from? Were other people with him?

Someone would come searching, sooner or later. They'd fly over and spot the body or whatever shiny metal he'd seen sliding down the hill below the body. He could run back to the still, bury the gin, hide his food, dismantle the place, and move to another canyon. But moving away would not guarantee that a search would miss him, whether he was here or somewhere new. An all-out manhunt could catch him in the net, too. He'd have to go miles from here, maybe even back into the maze district, to avoid detection.

"Gawdammit -- Nothing but trouble!" He shook

his musty beard.

The dust slowly dissipated and he put the lens to his eyes again. His ribs froze, unable to pull the air back into his lungs.

The leg had begun to swing back and forth.

CHAPTER 3

"Junk mail." Boss tossed the wrinkled envelopes in the trash and glanced at the clock. Seven-twelve. The sun was already heating the air in the living room he used as an office. Dog eared maps stood upright in the far corner. An expired notary public certificate hung on the wall behind his wooden desk. A worn leather couch blocked the front door, which he kept locked with two sets of dead bolts.

"Boss?" Harold stood out back by a sagging screen door, its frame held together with brackets and forty years of yellow paint. He called again and tapped on the nearby kitchen window.

"Come on, in here." Boss rubbed his thumb over the steel barrel of the .38 he kept in his desk drawer, then spun and inspected the loaded cylinder. His fingers encircled the grip and bobbed the Old West pistol like a trusted hand shake.

Harold crossed the worn kitchen linoleum and entered the living room through the internal doorway. He went straight to the closest chair across from the desk. He'd been Boss' lieutenant for more than five years and could gauge the man's moods like a barometer. He knew to sit quietly today.

Boss looked up and nodded. His nose hung like a drunken chili pepper, pale blue eyes in stark contrast to his sun-reddened skin. A "pit boss" for a few years at archeological sites across the southwest, the nickname had stuck. He'd made sure of it. He rubbed this thumb along the barrel of the pistol. He and Harold sat quietly.

"Hey, Boss, you here?" Roy thumped loudly through the back door and into the kitchen. He tucked dirty blonde hair behind his ears and pulled his baseball hat on tighter. His sparrow eyes darted about, moving quickly from object to object. Mr. Coffee gurgled from the countertop and Roy turned toward it. "Mind if I get some coffee?"

Harold and Boss exchanged a glance.

"Help yourself," Boss said and tucked the pistol away.

Roy came into the room sipping a white mug with a big, red "U" and sat next to Harold.

"Morning, morning," Roy nodded to each. He pushed a loose strand of hair from his eyes.

"Good morning, Roy." Boss's marbled eyes narrowed. "Anybody know you're meeting with me this morning?"

"No, 'course not," Roy grinned.

"Wives and girlfriends think you're somewhere else?"

"Helping a pal switch out an alternator on his pickup," Roy said.

Harold nodded an approval.

"Before we get going today there's something I need to show you guys." Boss stood, fists resting on the desk.

"What is it? You got a new find for us?" Roy looked expectantly at Harold, then Boss.

"It's more fun to show you." Boss grinned crookedly. "Let's go." He led them through the kitchen and took a cowboy hat from a peg by the door. "Out back."

Roy followed Boss and Harold trailed behind.

"Hey," Roy said, tugging his cap and turning to Harold. "Catch the game last night?"

"No."

"You're kidding! What a great game man, back and forth, back and forth, 26 to 28, then 30 to 32, Jazz behind, then they pull it off, at the end, four seconds to spare!"

"Out here by the backhoe." Boss led them about two hundred yards to a piece of sandstone the size of a dump truck. Behind it sat a rusted, orange backhoe by a pile of dirt and a trench nearly seven feet deep and eight feet long.

"You digging for gold now, Boss?" Roy peered over the edge. Boss nodded to Harold, who moved quickly behind Roy and shoved him.

"Whoa!" He twirled his arms as he slid over the edge, tossing his coffee ahead of him, then rolled when he hit. After a moment, he jumped up, his face flushed and taught.

"Harold - you son of a bitch - what the hell is wrong with you?" He began dusting himself off. "Give me a hand out of here! God, you're such a numb nuts."

Boss walked to the edge of the pit. "Roy, I'm afraid we've got some bad news for you." He said it like he was ordering dry toast for breakfast.

Roy froze, his mouth slightly open.

"Seems you've been skimming from me, selling artifacts on the side." Boss clucked his tongue.

Roy shook the hair out of his eyes. "Wait, Boss, no-no, no."

Boss pulled the pistol from his belt and checked

the cylinder. "You violated my trust, Roy."

"No, Boss, no..." he raised his arms as if he could stop the bullet.

Boss aimed casually, fired three rounds and waited until the sound echoed away. He watched to make sure Roy moved no more. He took a breath and turned to Harold.

"Never did like that coffee mug." Boss's lips curled in a grin.

Harold grunted and gave a quick smile.

"Take his car back to a public lot near town, lock it, toss the keys in the trash. The Sage Hotel's a good spot. Walk to the diner and have someone take you home from there."

Harold nodded.

"But first, fill this in." Boss looked up at the backhoe and pointed. "Then park it on top."

CHAPTER 4

Ethan woke reluctantly. Gradually, he felt the burn of flesh stripped of its skin, bruised ribs and throbbing temples. Everything hurt all at once. He considered opening his eyes, then thought better of it. He couldn't bear to think he was dead, though he most certainly must be. If he was not, he was in a ride through purgatory, half-alive and excoriated. He tried to inventory his parts, fearing whether they were mangled or even there at all.

He twitched his fingers – maybe a good sign. He rolled his shoulders and moaned as they resisted. He knew his legs were attached to his body because they felt like they'd been beaten with a baseball bat. His eyelids opened a crack and let in some light.

Sandstone seemed to hover above him. Was he upside down? After a moment, he sat part-way up, then collapsed back and gasped for breath.

"I wouldn't try moving too much, if I was you."

The coarse voice startled him. He rolled onto his left elbow and tried to focus.

"I'm amazed you're alive after that stunt. You should lay still till we get you cleaned up and checked out."

"Where the hell am I?"

"You're in my private quarters, is where. About 700 feet up and three miles from the river. About as high as you can go in this little canyon."

The answer made little sense to Ethan. "How did I end up here? And who are you?"

"Well, you'll have to figure out how you got most of the way here... I half carried and half dragged you from a ledge up there. I think you took a flying leap off the slick-rock trail, but don't ask me how you did it. Or how you lived through it." Relic tossed Ethan's hat to him. "Found this. Not much else."

Ethan closed his eyes. "Who are you, again?" His mind began to clear, but with it came a biting pain.

"Relic."

Did he hear "Relic"? "Thank you."

"Don't get all grateful. You've crashed my little enterprise here and I don't know quite what to do with you. Course, I might already have wounded you for life just moving you down that slope and into the shade. Here, take a drink, but not too fast."

Ethan opened his eyes, took the plastic bottle and drank deeply of fresh, cool water. A chill filled his stomach as he swallowed more.

"That's enough for now, plenty more when you're ready. Now, see if you can sit up."

Though his knees refused to bend, Ethan was able to swivel to the side. He realized he was on a soft mattress tucked against the corner of a shallow cave. He wiggled his feet off the cushion and leaned gingerly against smooth rock.

"Here, take a sip of this." Relic handed him a plastic cup of clear liquid.

The tart taste of gin made him cough. He slurped small amounts into his mouth, swished them around, and swallowed. Soon, he was finishing the cup in haste. His stomach warmed then burned like fresh jalapenos on a virgin tongue. He stared at the empty cup and pondered the magic he'd just ingested.

"More?"

"Yes. Please. Is it gin?"

"My own special recipe. Have another cup, then we'll clean you up some."

Ethan drank half of it in one swallow then sat still for several minutes. A warmth spread though his arms and legs. He started to suck a deep breath, but his ribs protested. His neck began to loosen and he stretched it cautiously. He could move his knees more easily and shifted to a more comfortable position then patted his chest and waist and looked himself over. His fanny pack, water bottle, and jacket were gone. He reached for his rear pocket.

"Shit, my wallet's gone."

"You'll have to get yourself a new one."

"My money, my license, my credit cards… damn."

"Watered down version of a medicine bag, an elder told me once. Your power, your identity, what allows you to move around in this world. I didn't see it anywhere. You'll have to get a new one when you get back to civ-il-i-zation."

Who is this guy? Ethan wondered. He looked past the rock shelter and across a span of country ever hazier behind each ridge of sandstone. They seemed to be high, but not quite to the tops of the most distant cliffs. They seemed to be a tiny point in the universe with a line of sight to infinity.

Ethan slowed his breath and refocused on the little camp. He had a hundred more questions but tried to start with just one. "What are you doing all the way out here?"

"You're kind of a nosy trespasser, aren't you?"

"Oh, oh, so sorry." Had he offended him? Ethan glanced at the man's impassive face, tanned dark by desert sun. A wiry beard hid his chin and reminded him of a country musician, but he couldn't think of his name. In fact, he wasn't sure just what to think at the moment. He tried another approach.

"Hey, thanks again for the gin -- what a relief it is to have it. But I'm confused. One minute I'm biking off trail, then…"

"Yeah, I found your bike. What's left of it."

"Shit. I'll lose my deposit on that."

"You're lucky you didn't lose your deposit on life. I'd say your spirit just about got evicted for good this afternoon."

"Where's the bike?"

"I had to bury it."

"Bury it?"

"Gave it a damn fine funeral too." Relic's lips curled in a quick grin.

"Why bury it?"

"Somebody's bound to come looking for you, sooner or later. If they use a spotter plane, the metal will flash at them miles away. It's best we keep you hidden 'till you – and I – can walk on out of here."

Ethan decided not to ask why or what this weathered, dusty man was hiding – it seemed safer not to know. Besides, if Relic had wanted to harm him, he needed only to have left him alone.

No one expected Ethan for a week. This was his vacation-adventure, seven days in the desert to ride, hike, float the river and cruise the bars. Shit. The rental place won't miss the bike for a week. Even then, if they remembered what trail he'd started on, he'd gone off trail, closer to the rim for a better look. The canyons were magnificent, the views so distant and wide they were hard to comprehend.

"I don't know how it happened," Ethan said. "Maybe something on the bike slipped up. I thought I hit the brakes, but then, maybe it was too late. I thought I had plenty of room to the edge."

"Sometimes these canyons will fool you. Distances look greater than they are, cliff edges blend in with the rocks below it."

Ethan held out the cup. "Do you mind?"

"Well, if you're gonna drink up all my profit I may as well get drunk with you." Relic poured them each a cup then sat on a rock near the edge of the shade.

"Sorry. I'll pay you back."

Relic waved him away and tossed back his drink.

Talking felt good to Ethan; he could do it without much movement. It confirmed his own sense of consciousness, too, something he wasn't ready to give up. "Your name is Relic?"

"Nickname. Nothing valuable about me, though."

Ethan nodded. "I've never been out here before, to this country." He swallowed more gin. "I'm from Bloomington, Illinois." He thought of his off-campus, basement apartment, and his roommate Donny. They called it the dungeon, and the name certainly fit. Maybe he should have stayed there on his stationary bike, pedaling away to nowhere. At least he'd be in one piece.

"Where are you from?" Ethan asked.

"Here and there, but I live here."

"How do you survive?" Ethan looked around the strange camp. A withered table topped with tools and plastic storage boxes stood near the shiny still. What looked like camping gear was piled by the back wall, next to a row of glass bottles filled with clear liquid – maybe gin. A pot of juniper berries rested on the ground near the still. The rock floor was surprisingly level and looked like it'd been swept. Dusty hiking boots, their dog-tongues loose and limp, were parked at the natural entrance to the camp.

"You live here all the time?"

Relic refilled his cup and took another long swallow. "I live here and there, all over. This is one nice place but I've got others. There's a spring just below here. Beyond that, there's an old moonshiner's camp the river tourists sometimes hike up to see."

"Really? How do you do it? I mean, how do you survive, eat and drink and live out here?"

"Pretty nosy for a guy who just missed dying, aren't you?"

"Sorry, I just think, well I just…"

Relic leaned forward, his arms on his knees, and looked intently at Ethan. "Let's get this over with."

Ethan's breath froze. "What do you mean?"

"Let's start with the worst of it. We've got to clean those wounds and it's going to hurt like the devil."

Ethan had surrendered, gratefully, to the gin and resented the reminder about his injuries. His short pants were shredded to almost nothing on his left hip, his legs red and swollen. Skin had been peeled off in long, thin tendrils the length of his right leg. His right arm was lacerated in places. His biking gloves were missing, but they must have protected his hands, which were only lightly scratched. He had no idea what his face or back looked like. His light jacket was gone but his T-shirt seemed to be intact. He wanted to fall asleep in an alcohol stupor. Really, was that too much to ask?

Relic lifted the edge of Ethan's shredded pants and began to pour home-made gin all over his legs.

Ethan shrieked like a falcon, then collapsed.

CHAPTER 5

Harold spread his leathery hands on the topographical map and stared at it. Boss popped the top on his beer and took a long swallow. An air conditioner hummed in the side window of the living room-turned-office. Faded lemon curtains were drawn across the picture window, lending the room a jaundiced glow.

"Horse Canyon." Boss said. "The upper branch of it. See here?" His thick finger pointed to the north drainage, which extended a mile or more from the river and ended in what appeared to be a box canyon.

"Where, exactly, did your nephew find the sandal?" Harold asked, his hazel eyes squinting at a dotted line that marked the center flow for spring run-off.

"Bobby said it was here," Boss rubbed his finger on the map, "just below the end of the canyon, in the sandy part of the dry creek."

"It looks small on the map, and it'll be a bitch to find on the ground. It's a lot of area. We'll have to do a lot of digging," Harold said.

"Sure enough. I want you to pack for seven or eight days. Raft down and camp somewhere private, away from the beach along the river."

"Tourists will start to be there pretty soon." Harold rubbed his chin.

"Already are. They started early this season, it's been so dry. Of course, you need to steer clear of them."

"Sure."

"You'll have to grid this somehow," Boss pointed again to the arroyo. "Dig and sift in ten or twelve foot squares, so you can do one grid at a time, maybe two or three a day, and refill the pit before you leave. In case anyone comes along."

Harold nodded.

"The camo tarps are on the back porch. Take them with you when you leave. You'll need extra batteries for your lights. And I want you to take Trevor and Bobby with you, this trip."

"Your nephew?" Harold raised his brow.

"Bobby's ready and he's got a strong back. And he knows right where he found the sandal." He faced the map but his eyes slid over to Harold.

"Oh, sure, no problem." Harold took a breath. "You talked to him about this, right?" He asked. "You know, what to do, what not to do, the ins and outs?"

Boss turned and stared.

"Of course you did, Boss. Just checking. Want to be thorough, right?" He nodded.

"Sure. I want you to be thorough. And Harold…" he put a fist on the table. "I want all three of you to bring pistols, just in case."

"I always do."

"Well, I want each of you to have one. This is an important site, could mean a lot of money for all of us. Don't get reckless but don't let anyone interfere, either. We have to get all we can this trip."

"Yes?"

Boss tightened his lips. "Don't forget about Roy, Harold. He sold us out to somebody and they just might know about this site. We may not get another chance, so… I want you working with military precision." He stood straight and clasped his hands behind his back, pleased with his choice of words. "This could put us all ahead, Harold, way ahead."

Harold nodded and stared at the map.

"And, one more thing. There's a twenty percent bonus in it for each of you, for whatever you bring back."

Harold grinned a row of uneven teeth.

CHAPTER 6

Rain patted into the dust and the earthen smell of wet sandstone filled the camp. Heavy clouds made the afternoon seem like nightfall. Ethan sat up and combed his fingers though his hair. A water bottle lay next to him, so he scooped it up and swallowed large gulps of water. He wiped his mouth with the back of his hand and looked around.

Relic stirred something in a pot on the old table, his back to Ethan. "You awake?"

"Yeah." He forgot where he was for a moment. "Yeah, I'm up." He scratched behind his ears and shifted to rest his back on the rock wall. His skin felt tighter than a mummy's and prickled with pain. He pulled his knees close to his stomach and examined his legs. Threads of dark maroon crisscrossed his thighs and calves, hard and scabbed, but not infected. His arms were worse in some patches, better in others. He rotated his wrists and wriggled his fingers and toes. Everything seemed to work slowly, but well enough.

"How long have I been sleeping?"

"All last night, but you woke up a lot, and into this afternoon."

"God, I'm starving."

"That's a good sign. I figured you'd be hungry today." Relic ladled boiled beans, chopped beef jerky and jalapenos onto a flour tortilla and rolled it into a burrito. He put it onto a hard plastic plate and brought it to Ethan.

His mouth watered at the smell of beans and peppers. "Oh my god, thank you." He brought the food to his face and bit chunk after chunk until his cheeks were full.

Relic made himself a burrito too, and sat in the folding camp chair at the foot of Ethan's bed. The rain began to lighten into mist and fade away. A cool breeze gave Ethan a brief chill.

They ate without speaking until Ethan was finished. He drank lustily of the cold water and belched.

"Want more?"

"I've never been so hungry in my life."

"You're on the mend. Your body is craving it." Relic set his unfinished food on the chair, went to the table, and made another helping for Ethan.

Soon, Ethan was finishing his second burrito. "I've never tasted anything so delicious."

"Edward Abbey said hunger is the greatest sauce of all. I guess if you're hungry enough, even my stuff's not so bad."

"Oh, man, stomach shock," Ethan said. He took shallow, measured breaths.

Intense brown eyes peered from Relic's weathered face and a smile crossed his lips. He seemed more relaxed than he had been yesterday.

"So tell me – how am I doing? You were putting alcohol on my cuts last night, weren't you?" Ethan said.

Relic nodded and stroked his wiry beard. "Several times through the night, half a jug's worth in all. You passed out the first time I poured it on you. But it's done the trick."

"What did the trick was drinking that stuff. Gin, right? That's good shit there, uh…"

"Relic."

"Relic." Ethan remembered.

"Well, it's way past noon and we're not going any-where. Want a pull of that gin?"

"Absolutely. But first, where does a guy take a leak

around here?"

"Down the trail to your left," Relic pointed, "any-where, but keep it a good distance. If you keep going you'll see the makeshift outhouse. Kind of an outhouse, only without the house."

Ethan turned and stood slowly. Lightheaded, he felt his way along the back wall, out from the shelter and down the narrow trail. When he got back, Relic had cleaned up the plates and covered the food.

Ethan crossed his legs and lowered gently into a seated position on the edge of the mattress. The short walk had left him winded and he sighed with relief.

"It hurts like hell to stand up and move."

"Best to keep moving tomorrow so you don't stiffen up." Relic handed Ethan a cup of gin and sat in the chair.

The thunderstorm had broken, revealing strips of clear blue sky. Ethan felt the drink warm his stomach again and the soreness in his muscles began to numb. Relic refilled their cups.

"How did you get the name Relic?"

He pulled the band from his crow-black hair and let it hang loosely across his shoulders. Tendrils of gray flowed from the top of his head. "It's a nickname. Guess my friends think I'm a relic."

"How so?"

He shrugged. "Because I live simple here. No computers, no cell phones, no phones at all. No internet, no GPS, no television." His voice was deep and serious.

"Man, you saved my life, Relic. I really want to thank you."

"Don't mind that. Just lucky I was here when you came flying in." He grinned. "Most folks use an airplane."

"Yeah." Ethan stared at his hands and thought about the fall. What terror it was to be flung into space, to lose all anchors, all control, all measure of time, everything but the realization you're going to die. And then, he didn't. He had no explanation for it. He finished his gin and held his cup out.

Relic poured another for them both. "You look a little concerned there, brother. Something on your mind?"

"Sure. I was just thinking about how I went over the ledge, how fast it happened. I was riding along the rocks, went down a steep slope, then right off." He slashed his palm through the air. "I had no idea I was that close to the edge. I could have died right then and there."

"Death can happen to anyone." Relic smiled. "Anytime."

"I know, I mean, yes, in theory you know it will." Ethan took another long drink. "But when it nearly happens to you, really, up close and personal, you have to think hard about it."

"Indeed." Relic took a sip. "And what do you think about it?"

"I think I haven't lived long enough yet, I haven't figured out what I'm doing yet, you know, the meaning of it all." The alcohol was coursing through his brain.

Relic nodded.

"I don't really know anything yet." He scraped his thumbs together nervously. "I'm serious, man. I haven't figured out what life is about, if I have a spiritual path. I know that sounds hokey. Hell, I don't know what's in my future, whether I have a future, a home, a girlfriend, a job, a life. I'm not ready to die. Not yet."

Relic ran his long fingers through his beard and looked at the ceiling of rock. "You know," he leaned forward, "an elder, someone you might call a medicine man, once told me that in this world, we're not human beings in search of a spiritual experience." He closed his eyes and shook his head. "Nope."

Ethan looked up at him.

"We are spirits, having a human experience."

CHAPTER 7

"Did you get the envelope?" Boss held the phone between his cheek and shoulder. He'd sent two photographs by mail to his contact in Atlanta, no return address, no letter, nothing written.

"I wish you'd send things by email," the distant voice said.

"You're not careful enough, bud. Government's got ways of hacking your emails, reading all your Facebook shit. All that computer crap is a trail of evidence leading you right to the Pen." Boss took a long swallow of cold beer. "What do you think?"

"It's a fine piece, no doubt." The man in Atlanta had done his research. This was no mere sandal from a local tribe, valuable as that was. This had a hide sole, probably of llama or goat leather. It had subtle design features of Aztec footwear too, but he was not about to tip off his seller.

"No shit. The leather is still intact and parts of the top are, too. You can see how the straps held the sandal on the foot." Boss tore at the paper label on his beer and waited.

"Agreed. What do you want for it?"

"Fifty."

"Fifty? I can't do fifty. More like thirty."

"I can go into the forties, but that's it."

"Thirty-five."

"Forty-five."

"Oh, hell, I'll go thirty-seven five, but that's it. If you had a matched pair, that would be another thing. Matched, I could go forty-five each, but I've not seen a decent pair of sandals in a decade."

Boss smiled. He knew his contact could get seventy thousand for an Anasazi sandal if he found the right buyer. But the markets in Atlanta and Miami were well out of Boss's reach. "Thirty-seven five it is."

"Is there more where this came from?"

He pushed his beer aside. "Oh, yeah."

"Tell me what you can."

"My nephew found this last year, just before winter set in. I know where to find more. My guys have already left for the site, a full expedition, as a matter of fact."

"Good."

"Give me a few weeks. There's bound to be more and the spot is real remote. It's not marked on any of the archeology maps, so it's not likely anybody else knows about it yet."

"A fresh source?" The Atlanta contact tried to mask his excitement.

"Yeah, fresh. Lots to check out. Maybe the missing one, too, so you'll have a pair. But expect the price to go up."

"Sure, if it's a match. But are you sure the site is just yours? No competitors, are there?"

"Nope."

"Your nephew will keep it quiet?"

"No problem there." And none of your business, Boss thought.

"Look, I don't doubt you, but I have to say, there's a dealer in Sarasota whose been getting some nice Southwestern stuff lately. Museum quality. You've got some competition out there, like it or not."

Boss remembered Roy trembling in the pit, shielding his face in foolish and futile panic. Of course, Roy had sold what he'd skimmed to someone else. Boss cleared his throat. "That stuff could come from anywhere in a thousand square miles. Nobody knows these canyons like my guys."

"Sure, no problem. Keep me posted and I'll prime my collectors. There's nothing like the promise of a matching pair of these, or of more to come."

"Let's do what we did last year. UPS half the cash to my house in town. I'll send the item to you the next working day. Then send the rest of the cash, same way."

"Fine by me. Good doing business with you."

"You too." Boss hung up the phone and finished his beer. He pulled a thin notebook from the bottom desk drawer and made a simple note on the unmarked column he used for gross revenue: 37.5. He was on his way to a banner year.

CHAPTER 8

The last pink light of sunrise faded to a pale blue and the smell of cowboy coffee prickled Ethan's nose. Three nights of gin-cleansed wounds and mild stupor left him sluggish but remarkably rested. He sat up and took a long and gluttonous drink of cool spring water.

The still had been disassembled, its parts lain neatly against the back wall of the cave. A row of metal ammunition boxes, locked shut, rested in a shallow hole. Relic stuffed items into a large camo day-pack and set it on the ground next to the table.

Ethan rubbed his eyes. "Coffee smells great."

Relic turned. "Help yourself." He took the blackened pot off a thin layer of hot coals and set it in the sand.

Ethan stood up and went to the table, where he found a bag of stale onion bagels and a mug. He blew sand out of the mug and poured himself a cup of coffee.

He lowered himself into the folding camp chair and tore off a piece of bagel.

Relic covered the ammo boxes with sand and smoothed the surface. He then dug a hole for the coals and buried them as well. When he was done, the only evidence of fire was a spot of smoke colored roof at the edge of the cave.

"What's going on? Why are you breaking camp?" asked Ethan.

"Time for me to move along and for you to find your way back home." Relic sat cross-legged on the ground in front of Ethan. "You're healing up real well, and I'm done here for a while."

Ethan washed down a chunk of bagel with warm coffee. He took a slow breath. "I suppose you're right, but where do I go now? Without your help, I'm lost."

"Easy, really. Let me show you." Relic wiped the ground with his hand and began to draw in the dust.

"Here's the river, here," he pointed. "It's maybe three miles down the drainage from where we are now. This time of year, rafters come past this canyon maybe once a week, once every two weeks. There's a nice beach and camping area where this canyon meets the river." He drew a long, winding line from the river toward their cave. "Just down from here is the spring, as you know, then below that a few hundred feet is an old timer's still. It's what's left of a still and old supplies and a rock shelter. Below that is a stone wall built by the moonshiners to ambush any revenuers dumb enough to chase them up canyon. The tourists – the rafters – like to come to the old still when they camp by the river."

Ethan leaned forward.

"I'm gonna give you my extra water bottle with a filter. At the river, fill the bottle, but you drink it through the filter. You'll never run out of water." Relic grinned through is stringy beard. "There's about 1,200 cfs this time of year."

"Cfs?"

"Cubic feet of water per second. It's how you measure water flow." Relic shook his head. "Anyway, you'll have plenty to drink. Wait there at the beach, where the arroyo meets the river and you'll have a rafting group come by sooner or later. They can feed you and take you out."

"Are you sure?"

"Sure as shit, there'll be a tourist group come along in a week or so. Maybe one there right now."

Ethan finished his coffee. "I hate to ask you this, with all the help you've given me already, but how will I eat?"

"Water's the main thing, Ethan. For food, I can spare a couple of bagels. If you ration yourself, you won't starve. Eat a half of one a day, drink lots of water, stay rested and you'll be fine."

"I can't go with you, I guess..."

Relic shook his head. "Here, let me show you the rest of the canyon here..." He drew another line from the river roughly parallel to the first line he'd drawn, then drew it away on another track.

"This canyon is really two separate ones that meet up at the river. Where we are now is the main drainage, the south one. We're about as high up this side canyon as a man can go.

"Then, there's another drainage to the north of us. At the river, there's only one trail but it quickly divides into two – the north drainage and the south one." He drew more marks in the dust. "Here we are, here's the old moonshiner's still, here's where the north and south trails come together. If you go up the north trail, it peters out but you can go on up the drainage quite a bit farther, a couple of miles, before you hit a box canyon. There's a seep there, a small spring, in case you are in that area and need water."

Ethan studied the map closely. "And you're sure it's not better to go back the way I came, maybe see if another mountain biker could find me?"

Relic snorted. "There is no way in hell you can get back up there. You took a flying leap off the edge, remember? No way up it without climbing ropes and a whole lot of help."

Ethan sighed. "OK."

"Here, where the trail hits the river, just this side of the beach is a set of ancient Pueblo ruins. Tourists stop to see these a lot, too. There's a row of four stone houses and several granaries, where they stored corn and beans and meat for the winter."

"Here?" Ethan pointed.

"Right." Relic looked at Ethan sternly. "Don't go inside them or touch them. They're 1,000 years old and easily get messed up. I can't tell you how many times I've seen tourists damage these sites."

"Got it."

"Another thing. If you see any petroglyphs, look but don't touch them, either. Even the small amount of oil in your skin can transfer to the rock and break it down faster than nature intended."

Ethan nodded. "Where are the petroglyphs?"

"They are all over these canyons, including some places you wouldn't expect." Relic seemed to think about something for a moment. "I'll tell you two more things.

Some of these petroglyphs we can read today. If you find them, you'll see one in each of these drainages, the north one and the one we're in, that tell you water is available up the trail. They look like this…" Relic drew a spiral and a wavy line above it. "It tells you to go up, and you can find water. And there's another one that's important you might see along the trail to the river."

Relic drew a stick figure with a round circle in front of it and dots below. "There's a way to get from one drainage to the other without going all the way back to the river. There's a spot on both trails, maybe half-way up each one, where you can cross over. Here…" He drew a bending line connecting the north and south drainages. "A similar petro is on the north trail, showing you where to start up. There's no trail there. You have to bushwack it and cross some large, bare rocks. You can get lost up there, so I don't recommend it. But if you keep your general bearings, you can reach the other trail."

"What does this petroglyph mean?" Ethan pointed to the stick figure.

"This is a person, of course. I think this circle in front of him is a war shield, myself. The dots seem to represent a way forward. Not really a path, but a way you can cover the ground from the south drainage to the north one, or vice versa."

"Wow. So, the tribes used these as trail markers?"

"Well, that's what I think." He leaned back and looked at Ethan. "Got it?"

"Yes, I think so." He stared at the map again, careful to memorize it. Then he looked at Relic, a hint of indecision in his eyes.

"You may as well ask me," Relic said with a wry grin.

"I don't know if I want to."

"Look, I'll tell you this. I'm not some axe murderer or something."

"I never thought that. I just wondered…"

"I've just got my own ways about me. I love living out here and there are a few folks not too happy to see me. So, I keep to myself. I like it that way. I got blue sky, red rocks, plenty of fresh air and places to explore. And enough gin to keep a man's blood red." He grinned.

"Thanks."

"One final thing." Relic's voice was low and serious. "You can't tell anyone about me – no one at all, no matter how much you trust them. You do owe me your life, son, and now I'm trusting you with mine. I'm a happy hermit, and I want to keep it that way."

"Of course. I'll tell no one. I'll just say my bike got damaged and I hiked down to the river."

"Exactly."

"No one will know, I promise." Besides, Ethan thought, who would believe him anyway?

"Well, then, time to go." Relic wiped the earthen map clean and stood up. "Help me roll up this mattress."

Ethan's wounds prickled as he rose to his feet. He clenched his teeth until the stinging passed.

They rolled and tied the mattress with twine and stuffed it and the folding chair behind the dissembled still. The legs of the table were metal pipes screwed into fittings on the wooden top. Relic detached the legs and laid the table parts with the still, then covered it all with a heavy canvas tarp. He placed rocks along the edges of the tarp to secure it. When he was done, the shallow cave looked completely natural but for the tarp, which blended well with the dark rock in the shadow of the sandstone ledge.

Amazing, thought Ethan. Ammo boxes with water, medicine, jerky, beans, spices, cookware, mugs and more lay beneath the sand, completely hidden. Bottles of gin lined the back wall, equally hidden in the cool sand. No one would notice the tarp unless they walked right up to it and touched it. Only then could they tell it was something other than smooth rock.

Relic shouldered his pack and carefully brushed their tracks out of the dust with a handful of rabbit brush.

They walked slowly down to the spring, a few yards away, where Relic finished and tossed the brush aside.

Ethan looked up. They had made a gentle turn on the way and the small cave was not visible from the spring. Nothing in that direction would entice anyone to scramble up there.

"Good luck to you, Ethan." Relic offered his hand.

"Thank you so much. Good luck to you, too." Ethan shook his hand. Relic turned and walked across the bare rock to the south, gone from Ethan's view within moments.

Ethan straightened his hat and checked his pockets for the bagels and borrowed water bottle. He filled it with water from the spring, then sat on his haunches for a few minutes, soaking in the view. Across the way stood a small, distinctive spire, maybe twenty feet high, with a band of light sandstone near its top. The tiny trail wound down and to his left.

Well, he thought, here goes.

CHAPTER 9

Ethan walked casually down along the rocks, wound past a house-sized boulder then came abruptly to a stone and mortar wall with a wooden door, hung crooked on rusted hinges. He'd found the old moon-shiner's place.

"I'll be damned." He felt along the rock wall and walked through the doorway. Inside sat a small wooden stove ringed by fallen pipes. A wooden bench sat toward the back wall, nails, empty cans, and various other pieces of rusted metal littered the area. A large opening faced out from the front of the structure, looking down the canyon trail beyond. Boards were attached to the top of the opening and pieces of leather still hung from them. Maybe it was an open-air window that could be closed with a large cow hide. The one-room structure was built into a shallow cave, not unlike the one Relic and he had used higher up. Natural rock provided the back wall and roof. Stones stacked like bricks formed the rest of the walls.

He walked back out of the small stone cabin and around to the other side, where all manner of tin drums, copper tubes, valves and odd parts lay scattered about: the old still, or what was left of it. From there the view opened to a wide area of the canyon. He could see the trail a mile or more into the distance, larger and more obvious than the narrow one above the spring. The cabin was in a perfect spot to watch for anyone coming up the canyon. He lingered for a while, inspecting the sparse living quarters, then started down again.

After a few hundred yards, he turned and glanced up and down the canyon. The distinctive spire he'd seen earlier was now above and behind him. The cabin was so well hidden he could barely make it out. If you didn't know where to look, you would have no idea it was there. To his right, across the gully, stood a row of hand-stacked rocks. He looked along the length of the trail. The rocks would make a good spot for an ambush, if the moonshiners were being chased.

He took a long drink of water. The sun was beating down on him already, and it was not yet noon. He thought of Relic's old mattress and how great a nap in the shade would feel.

The canyon spread into a wide and relatively flat area, filled with low bushes and small, purple flowers. Walking was easy for a while, until the canyon narrowed again and the trail wound its way through ankle-twisting rocks and boulders. He stopped for a moment to get his bearings. At the next bend in the trail was something barely visible on the wall of rock, hidden behind some sage. He went closer to inspect and there it was – the stick figure of a man with a shield in front of him and several dots pecked into the rock below him. The petroglyph, just as Relic had described it.

He stared at the figure for a while, thinking of the man who had etched it into the sandstone, maybe a thousand years ago. What had he been like? What had it been like to live here back then?

Just beyond the petroglyph, he could see a way to walk up the rock wall, a gentle slope you could follow up and over the nearest boulders. He went carefully up, holding onto the wall as he went, until he reached the nearest rim. Beyond that, he could see an easy way to keep going, along and across long stretches of solid rock that rounded off in the distance.

He remembered Relic's advice about getting lost up on this dome, and turned around. Back on the trail, he walked quickly down slope to another area where the vast canyon opened again. This time, he could see the mighty river and even the sheer cliff walls beyond it. He could dimly see what must be the campsite area, where tall cottonwoods hid the beach.

He quickened his pace and soon found himself within a mile of the river. The trail led him up and down, left, then right, then onto a ledge overlooking the trees and narrow strip of sand beyond. He caught his breath and surveyed the mouth of the canyon carefully, looking for signs of human life and a good spot to settle in. The hike was warming his muscles, muting the sting of abrasions on his legs.

To the north, he could see where the upper drainage trail connected to the one he was on. The north canyon seemed to go a very long way up, then around a bend and out of sight. He could tell where the gully continued by examining the cliffs above it.

Along the river, he could see flat open areas ideal for tents. Toward the south end of the trees, he thought he saw something blue, something man-made. He walked farther along the ledge, down a switchback and to another rim. There it was: a rectangular tent with what looked like camp chairs nearby. The area was small and secluded, a good distance from the trees and beach.

CHAPTER 10

His salvation, his ticket to food and rest, lay three-quarters of a mile away as the crow flies, and probably a mile away by trail. He started down the path again in earnest, hurrying as best he could, but careful not to trip.

The route disappeared over a flat section of rock and he lost it on the other side for a few hundred feet. He'd come out too high, so he crossed down to the trail again. It twisted along the dry creek bed, sometimes through it to the other side, sometimes along a bench above. A prickly pear cactus stung his right leg, reminding him to slow.

The path dropped steeply to a flat plain, then leveled out. He looked around for the people or their tent, estimating where they might be. He slid down a short slope into the dry bed where it opened level with the tall cottonwoods a quarter mile away. He must be close now; the tent should be level with him and to his left. He loped off the trail and into a patch of hip-high brush on flat ground. Winding his way through, he kept the cottonwoods on his right and kept going toward the river. There, off to his left, he could see part of the blue tent.

His heart quickened and he called out. "Hello! Anyone here?"

He slowed his pace and stopped at the front of a light blue and gray nylon tent staked in the sand. A couple of camp chairs and a fire pan sat about thirty feet from the tent. An opaque plastic container sat between the chairs, mugs and plates resting on top.

"Hello?" He yelled louder, but heard no response. He walked around the tent, where two more plastic storage containers sat with large rocks on top, presumably to keep the lids from blowing off.

"Well, shit. Nobody home." He walked around the tent again. Where would they have gone? The only choice along any path would be toward the cottonwoods and closer to the river, so he cut across a rock outcrop and back to the trail.

In short order, he was beneath the tall cottonwoods. Beyond that lay a crescent-shaped beach.

"Hey, anyone here?" He yelled into the trees. "Well," he said to himself, "they've gotta be back by nightfall."

He slipped off his shoes and walked across the sand to the coffee-colored river. Across the water stood a massive wall of blood-red sandstone streaked with dark varnish. He leaned back to see the top of the cliffs towering a thousand feet above him. High canyon walls extended up-stream and down as far as he could see, narrowing the sky above, secluding the river, and this spot, from the rest of the world.

He wiggled his toes into the warm sand as a short gust of wind blew from the north. He took off his hat, filled it with river water, and put it back on his head. Icy cold water ran down his neck and back and made him shiver, even in the afternoon heat.

He wandered aimlessly up the beach then turned back into the trees. Across the way, up a few feet higher, he saw the ancient rock houses Relic had told him about. One, then two, three, and four in a close row some distance away, all overlooking the river. He was staring at ancient history. Each one stood eight to ten feet high and had been molded to match the natural rock around them. One doorway was topped with a single, long rock. Other doorways were held up with long sticks, preserved in place by the desert for hundreds of years. As he went closer, he could see how mud had been packed between the stones. He looked carefully inside the largest one. A window on one side admitted a shaft of light that made it hard to see into the deep shadows. This one was about twelve by fourteen feet - cramped for the cold months, but plenty of room for summer living.

Some sections of wall were curved to fit the rock formations and others had sharp, squared-off edges perfect to his eye. He walked to the edge of the cliff toward the river and then turned around and went back along the ruins, past the four houses. Evenly spaced footholds were carved into the cliff at one spot and led him about twenty feet higher. Up there, a long rock structure was nestled under the ledge. It had a low entrance and no windows – a granary for storing food.

He walked carefully back down and explored the area farther up, toward the north drainage trail. He could see up the side canyon a few hundred yards before it twisted out of sight. Maybe the campers had gone up the canyon, but he lacked the ambition to find out. They'd be back, of that he was sure. And they ought to help him with food and water, too. At least, he hoped so.

Ethan was quickly tiring. He went back to a shady spot in the trees, ate half a bagel and drank the rest of his bottle of water. He leaned back into the soft sand, squirmed into place, and fell fast asleep.

CHAPTER 11

A throaty sound grew on the wind like the groan of a sleeping ogre. Anya put her weight into the oars again, feeling their pull and bend against the current, slipping the raft to the far right side of the river, expecting a series of rapids around the corner and dangerous rocks on the left.

Anya was lead guide on this river tour, her second year in the coveted role. She had four passengers on her raft and was still trying to remember their names. Norma, an older woman, sat in the back of the raft next to her teenage niece, Lisa. The young girl wore tiny ear-phones plugged into some hand-held device the size and thickness of a piece of fruitcake. Her face seemed magnetized to it. Carter, a young man with a Seahawks T-shirt, sat in front with a middle-aged man named Lars. She remembered Lars as the pudgy man with the yellow bucket hat.

Her fellow guide, Tim, rowed a second raft about seven hundred feet behind her. Tim's boat was loaded with camp supplies and two more guests, a married couple. He glanced at Anya, who nodded. Tim began to move his raft toward the right bank of the river.

Anya began to row again when a high pitched shriek turned all heads toward the sound. Lisa splashed in shallow water pooled in the bottom of the boat, flaying wildly.

Anya lifted the oars from the river and laid them on the sides of the raft. "What's wrong?"

"My music, it's in the water!" Lisa swung her arms like a panicked chimpanzee, sweeping them across the rubber floor.

Carter reached down and felt along his side of the raft, working his way from the bow to the center. "Hooray!" he announced, lifting the dripping device above his head.

"Oh, oh, let me have it," Lisa pled. He shook it and handed it to her.

Without a thanks, Lisa held it close to her chest and scooted close to her aunt Norma. "It slipped out of my hand," she said to no one in particular. "It happened so fast!"

"Honey, it's broken now," Norma said.

"No, no, I'll take it apart and dry it all out." Her skinny fingers pried open the shiny gadget and she shook it, and blew it, and wiped it again and again with her T-shirt.

Norma looked at Carter. "Thank you."

"Sure," he mumbled, distracted by the sound of water in turmoil. He looked up at Anya expectantly. "Rapids?"

She nodded. "Right around this bend."

Anya could sense Norma's anxiety as the rumble of whitewater grew louder. She knew that now was a good time for some reminders.

"Everyone, please pull on your life preserver straps. They can work their way loose sometimes, and we want them all nice and snug."

They did as they were asked, pulling, yanking, and testing their vests.

"This set of rapids is sometimes called Government Rapids because they shift around a lot every year, depending on the politics, I'm told."

Norma grinned at the weak joke.

"Anyway, we'll pass a run of large rocks on the left. They're the ones making all this noise."

Lars saw Carter grab the safety rope on the raft and followed his lead.

"Straight ahead is Sunset Wall," Anya pointed. "It's a solid sandstone slab almost a thousand feet tall and five hundred feet wide. You can guess how it got its name: it's a beautiful sight at sunset. The rapids are just beyond it."

Anya looked around the boat. The front and rear ends of the raft were inflated white tubes curved into semi-circles. Straight tubes connected each side of the raft at right angles, forming a rectangle in the center. All the tubes were full and tight. An aluminum frame was strapped to the inside of the tubes that formed the rect-angle. Anya sat on a wooden bench seat atop the metal frame, which held the rowlocks for the long oars. Their gear was all stored in rubberized "dry" bags strapped to the frame. She could see nothing lying loose in the boat. Anya pulled them farther toward the right shore.

"Like I said, we'll pass the first set of waves on our left. I'll row us center again and we'll dodge a couple big holes, then we're through. Remember to hold onto the ropes, like Lars is doing, but don't wrap the rope around your hands or your arms. If you need to let loose, you don't want to be tangled up."

She looked back at Norma and her niece.

"Tuck your feet between the side of the raft and the floor of the raft," she raised her voice above the noise. They turned the corner, spinning quickly past the rocky shore.

Wide awake, the ogre was now in a full-throated roar, drowning all sound but his own.

Brown water boiled into white caps spitting off massive boulders, rushing down into holes behind the rocks then rising up again in standing waves twelve feet high. Anya began to row them left again, toward the dangerous white caps, but knowing the current would move them safely downriver before they reached them. She needed to line up the raft for the next part of the run, closer to the center of the river. She watched the deep rapids sweep out of view, then quickened her efforts. The raft moved to the center of a smooth, v-shaped surface then raced into the second set of waves.

They hit the center rapid head on, dropping down, then flying up into the spray. Buckets of water hit Carter and Lars in the face and chest, shoving them back into the raft.

"Wu-woo!" Carter yelled.

Anya glanced at her passengers, making sure she still had four of them. The raft slipped downslope again on the next wave and tried to pirouette sideways but she rowed hard to keep them heading straight into the third wave.

The water took them up again quickly, spray filling the raft. Suddenly, Carter's body slid parallel to the boat. Anya could see him hanging on with both hands, but his feet had lost their grip. In a second, his legs were outside the raft.

Anya spun the raft toward Carter, helping to keep his momentum toward the boat, rather than away from it. Lars reached across and grabbed Carter's life preserver, tugging him in. Carter kicked his legs and squirmed on top of the slippery sidewall, Lars pulling again, Carter dumping into the bottom of the raft like a flopping catfish.

They dropped quickly into the next trough, which was shallower than the last. Carter got his legs beneath him and sat upright. He lodged his feet under the sides of the boat and tossed his dark hair out of his eyes. He seemed a little stunned, even pensive.

"Thanks, man," he said to Lars.

"Glad to help," Lars grinned.

Then adrenaline seemed to kick Carter into a higher gear. "That was incredible," he yelled and pounded the side of the raft. "Crazy, crazy, incredible!"

"You nearly swam that last rapid all by yourself," Anya grinned.

"Yeah!" Carter said to Lars, then shouted it again to the rolling waves.

Anya pushed the sunglasses higher on her nose. There are two types of people in the world, she thought: those who fear the rushing current and those who love it. But nobody rides the muscled river without respecting it.

CHAPTER 12

The chatter of friendly voices filled his dreams until he realized they were real. He sat up quickly and looked around, but saw no one. He heard only echoes. Then two large white and red rafts came into view, oared by figures atop a low platform in the middle of each boat. Four passengers sat in the lead raft, two in the second one. The creak of wooden oars mixed with the crisp voices. Soon he could distinguish words and he felt like Robinson Crusoe, rescued at last.

He watched as the river guides brought their boats to shore, ran out lines to the beach and pounded an anchor into the sand. A middle-aged man in a bucket hat and brightly-colored shirt slid awkwardly into the shallow water and waded ashore. A light-haired woman under a broad-rimmed hat stayed in the raft. She was packing and unpacking a small rubberized bag. A skinny girl next to her seemed not to notice anything, but eventually turned and slid out of the boat. He could see a resemblance; maybe the teenager was the woman's daughter.

The first guide hopped nimbly back into the boat and across the tied-in equipment. When the guide stood and stretched, the curve of her waist made it clear she was female. She adjusted the green baseball cap on her head and began to unhook dry bags and camp gear, tossing them to the shore or the front of the boat.

Ethan was maybe fifty feet away, in the cool shadows. The sun had dropped since he'd arrived; it was probably getting close to supper time. The thought made his stomach rumble.

He rose and brushed the sand from his clothes. "I wonder what I'll look like to these people?" he thought. "Robinson Crusoe," he smiled to himself. "Or worse."

He walked toward the boats and the man in the colorful shirt. Confusion appeared on the man's face, but he nodded. "Good afternoon."

Ethan nodded back.

"Ahoy!" Ethan yelled at the female guide, who stopped and gaped at him a moment. "Hello! Beautiful day."

"Yes, it is," Ethan came closer to the raft.

"Are you camped here already?" she turned toward

him. Her face and shoulders were broad, with a shining white smile to match. Mirrored sunglasses hid her eyes. A forest green hat with a petroglyph logo kept her dark brown hair back from her forehead. "I'm Anya." She skimmed over packs, pads and boards like a water skipper and hopped down to the sand to shake his hand.

"Nice to meet you." She looked at him more closely, concern in the wrinkles around her eyes. Her grip was firm and quick and she had the hardened muscles of a seasoned rafter.

"I'm Ethan." He felt lightheaded - he'd not had a drink in four and a half hours.

"Is this your campsite? Where's your boat?" Anya looked up and down the small beach.

"No, you see, I'm stuck here. I'm kind of in trouble."

"Are you OK?" She noticed the bruises and scabs on his arms and legs.

"Sort of. I was biking up on the rim, on the trails up there."

Anya took off her glasses. Her dark eyes sparkled like headlights. "Up top?"

"Yes, well, I was up top, but I went off trail for a bit and got going down a slope of rock and found out I was a lot closer to the edge than I thought. I went off the edge and crashed my bike."

"Oh, god."

"I came down and found a spring, so I holed up there for a bit, at that old still, under the ledge." He'd promised Relic to say nothing of him or his hidden still, which lie above the rusty one the visitors liked to see. "I'm out of food and water and came down to the river hoping to find some help."

"Whoa. Glad you made it down here, Ethan." She shook his hand again. "You're lucky you could travel all that way. Let's get you some water." She pointed to his empty water bottle and he handed it to her. She took it to an orange cooler strapped to the raft and filled it with melted ice.

"Thank you." He took a long drink and let the water drip from his chin. "That's incredible, thank you."

"Hey, no problem. You're welcome to hook up with us. We have more than enough food and water for the group. Why don't we introduce you around and get you something to eat."

Ethan took a deep breath and smiled. Relic had been right about finding help down by the river.

Anya climbed to the top of the raft and shouted for everyone to listen. "I want you to meet Ethan." She pointed at him. "He's had an accident biking on the rim trail and, somehow, he got himself down to the river safely. We have lots of extra food and water, and he needs a way out of these canyons and back to town. We're going to help him out, which is how we do things in the back country. He's going to join us for supper and the rest of the trip. Tim," she looked around, "get him something to eat and see what he needs for tonight: sleeping bag, fleece pants, jacket, that kind of thing. And see if he needs anything for cuts and bruises."

The other guide nodded and waved for Ethan to come closer.

"Everyone please give Ethan a big hello."

CHAPTER 13

Harold flung a drop of sweat from his nose and grabbed the towel. It felt like a hundred and five degrees in the shade. He dried his face and leaned on the shovel to rest. He'd finished back-filling one of the excavation pits and decided to catch his breath.

Bobby and Trevor were bent over in an open pit, sifting through dirt and rock for any sign of artifacts.

"You guys about done with that one?" Harold asked.

"Just about," Bobby said.

"No luck except bad luck," Trevor added without humor.

Bobby glanced at him like a sidewinder woken from a summer's nap. "You'll quit your whining when we find another sandal."

"You're right about that," Trevor sat on the edge of the square-shaped pit. "But for now I say we're all done

71

here." Trevor turned toward Harold and nodded.

Bobby dropped his trowel by the pile of dirt they'd removed and hopped out of the pit. He took a hand rag off an upright shovel and mopped his face and neck.

Harold turned quickly toward a steep hill across from the dig, listening intently. The sound of rock clacking on rock had been faint and distant, but real. Maybe a herd of mountain sheep, foraging for food up there. But only a lonely crow circled the hill.

"Let's call it a day and get back to camp," Harold twisted back toward the other men. "We can fill in these two pits in the morning."

"You don't have to tell me twice." Trevor pulled off his leather gloves and tossed them aside.

"I need some supper, but I want to come back and get another hour or two in before nightfall," Bobby put his hands on his hips.

"Suit yourself," Harold said, shaking his head. Damned twenty year olds.

Harold laid his shovel under the tarp and swept the surface of the closed pit with an old straw broom. The area still looked a little unnatural, but the next rain would hide it nicely. Bobby and Trevor finished putting away their gear.

A combination of fatigue and gravity pulled them

in uneven gaits slowly down the canyon.

Nearly a mile from their dig, they began to hear voices from under the cottonwood trees by the river. Tourists. A group of rafters had arrived. Without a word, they moved farther from the sounds, skirting the drainage on the far side and watching closely for wanderers from the herd.

The men eventually reached their tents, which were pitched on flat ground between sage brush and clumps of grass.

"We better move camp up toward those cliffs," Harold said quietly. "Don't be banging any pots and pans. And from now on, we'll have to keep one of us on guard at the site while the others work."

Bobby and Trevor grunted their reluctant agreement. They broke camp quickly and carried their gear to the cliffs about a quarter of a mile up river. A ten-foot overhang protected a sandy spot at the base of the sandstone which meant, thankfully, there was no need to set up their tents again. Bobby laid out his sleeping bag, set up the three camp chairs, and grabbed something for each of them to drink.

In the desert, warm beer and cold stew rival champagne and filet mignon. They let their frustrations fade as their stomachs filled and they were soon resting contently in the shade.

CHAPTER 14

The sun slid behind burnt red cliffs, leaving their stretch of canyon in cool evening light. Tim and Anya had cooked marmalade-basted chicken on a propane grill, with fresh green peppers, onion, and olives, apple cobbler for desert. One of the guests brought a box of chardonnay. Ethan had never lusted for food or eaten so well as this. Not even with Relic.

Ethan was trying to recall the names of them all. He'd met them earlier, of course, when Anya called them to the boat, but it was too much too fast. Since then, he'd watched them prattle about the beach, pitching tents, unpacking their dry bags, arranging their stuff, and taking pictures.

Anya and Tim were easy to remember. They were a marvel of efficiency, setting up tables, camp chairs, a cooking area, pots for washing plates and silverware, and even a porta-potty. Tim's long limbs exaggerated his knees and elbows, which pumped in all directions as he moved about the anchored raft. Anya had rower's shoulders and a desert tan. She wore what looked like a sports bra under a tank top and wore short pants with many pockets. Lisa was in her teens, he guessed, and came with her aunt or maybe her mother, he wasn't sure. Her shoulder length hair was ruined with streaks of harsh, artificial blonde, flashed like lightening on a dark cloud. She seemed to be fussing with some sort of gizmo.

He took a deep drink of water and looked upriver. A middle-aged man with short legs and a sagging tummy sat several yards away from the others. A yellow bucket hat covered his head. He was bent over, focused on some papers balanced on his knee. What would he be working on way out here?

Ethan stood and carried his camp chair up the beach. He wiggled it into the sand next to the man. "Mind if I join you?"

"Welcome." The man shuffled his papers into a waterproof bag and tucked them under his seat. "Lars," he said and held out his hand.

"Ethan." They shook hands.

"Did you like the meal?"

"God, yes," Ethan said.

"I was impressed too. This is my first trip into this kind of country." They listened to the river rolling past the boats.

"Well, you pretty much know my story, how I got here. What brings you on a whitewater river trip?" Ethan asked.

Lars shivered in the cool breeze and pulled his hands into his sleeves. "I have a friend who insisted I should go."

"Your friend didn't come with you?"

"No, he couldn't come. He couldn't spare the time. Neither can I, really, but I thought maybe it'd be therapeutic."

Ethan looked at him.

"I'm just now divorced, you see."

"Ah," Ethan said, as if he understood.

"We'd been married eight years, no children. Thank god, I guess. And I needed some time away from everything. My pal said you can't get more away from everything than in these canyons. Cell phones don't work, radios don't work, nobody comes or goes in here but in rafts or kayaks."

"Unless you come over the edge of a cliff, the hard way. Destroy your mountain bike. Nearly kill yourself," Ethan chuckled. "Roll your busted ribs all the way down to the river."

Lars's grin revealed a row of even but slightly over-crowded teeth.

"What do you do for a living, Lars?"

His smile dropped off like a weight.

"Sorry, man," Ethan nearly whispered.

Lars rubbed the palms of his hands like they were rubber gloves he could not loosen. "No, it's OK. I love my job, really, but it's… stressful."

Dusk had drained the sandstone walls of their heat and color, and harsh shadows disappeared. There was something private and comforting about the dark, like they were sitting in the booth of a quiet pub, where the glare and judgment of other humans was muted. Ethan watched him expectantly.

"I'm vice president for product development and marketing at Vestco Insurance. I'm sure you've heard of us."

"The one with the talking horse? The TV ad where the horse talks about cheap rates then orders a pizza?"

"That's us." He grinned at the dust at his feet. "Sounds funny but the job is never ending. I've been at it for seven years now without a break. This trip is the first one. I work nearly eighty hours a week, every week. Well, I did have Christmas eve and Christmas morning off this year."

"Even a horse has to stop and smell the pizza."

Lars smiled and looked up. "Yeah, thanks. Anyway, it's a blur of meetings with people who can't get along or riddle their way out of a wet paper bag, stats, stats and more stats. Who cares when your love life goes to shit? Who cares as long as your suits are clean and you keep your numbers up and the damn horse laughs and orders the goddamn pizza? And my president," his hands began kneading themselves again, "is a sneaky son of a bitch who only cares about how good we make him look. And whether he gets his bonus each year. It took me years to figure out what now seems so damn obvious. And we have a board of directors who expect loyalty to the death."

"After flying off the canyon wall, I say no one has the right to demand that from anybody."

"You know, you are right." His face seemed to ossify into a colorless statue.

"So, why not take a long break? Quit for a while. Take a deep breath and get reoriented."

Lars looked up at Ethan with a hint of confusion, and a bit of incredulity. "But… I've worked hard to work this hard," he replied, not a hint of irony in his voice.

CHAPTER 15

"Coffee!" Tim yelled at the camp and clanged the heavy pot with a spoon.

Sunlight flashed on a small triangle of cliff high above them and unrolled like a rug, exposing rust-orange rock and streaks of black varnish that dripped from the rim. Ethan blinked at the sky and wiggled out of the patched-up sleeping bag that had kept him warm.

The rest of the crew was soon up and eating, chatting, washing up or just visiting with each other. A married couple, he'd try to think of their names, sat with Lars. The husband seemed to be in his forties, fit and trim, as was his wife. Both had sky blue eyes and Nordic features. Darren and Millie, that was it. They spoke nervously but seemed comfortable in expensive camping gear that looked new. Ethan glanced at his partially shredded hiking shorts and smiled. At least they covered what they needed to.

Norma wore her blonde-gray hair pulled tight in a ponytail and tucked behind her ears. Ethan stopped to say hello. Norma had come on a river trip many years ago and thought it would be good to bring Lisa out into the canyon country. Norma was a pleasant person, but behaved more elderly than she appeared. Maybe she was in an endeavor – dealing with her niece – that was just beyond her reach.

After breakfast, Tim stood on an upturned plastic bucket and shouted: "Everyone, gather 'round!"

Carter shuffled across the beach and the married couple stood up together. Everyone trotted closer.

"Everyone get enough to eat this morning?" Nods and smiles all around. "Good, cause today we're going to wear it all off of you by noon," Tim grinned. "We have a great hike planned up the south side of the canyon today. We'll see petroglyphs, walk under the cliffs, and stop at a beautiful little spring and an old moonshiner's still, hidden along the trail. For those of us too young to know, prohibition was a time in this country when drinking alcohol was outlawed by the U.S. Constitution. Ironically, the State of Utah, where alcohol is strictly regulated today, helped end prohibition in 1933.

"Revenuers came up this canyon during prohibition. They knew there was someone brewing alcohol because it was coming into nearby towns by the case-full. Just a few months before the end of prohibition, they had a famous shoot out up there. The moonshiners could see them coming, and ambushed the revenuers, driving them away. Later, the sheriff and revenuers came back in force and found the stills abandoned. They destroyed the stills with axes and generally trashed the rock cabin where the moonshiners stayed. We'll see the old stills, and what's left of the cabin and supplies up near the spring, which is where they got their water for the operation.

"This is a full day hike, up and back. You're welcome to stay here with Anya if you like. Those coming with me should bring plenty of sun-screen and a full water bottle. We have gorp, candy, and granola on the table, and that's what's for lunch today. When we get back, Anya will have salmon or hamburgers for supper, whichever you prefer."

"How about both?" Carter said.

"You bet. We've already talked about the basic principle of back country hiking and camping. If you bring it in, pack it out."

"Even poop?" Carter smiled.

"Even poop. If you can't wait to poop till we get back to camp, I have toilet paper and plastic bags for your use. So, a reminder, please leave behind no candy wrappers, tissues, or trash of any kind. If you see that someone else has dropped some trash, please pick it up and bring it back to camp, where you can throw it out here. Anyone who needs to use the bathroom, please do so before we go. Let's leave here in about fifteen minutes. Don't forget your cameras."

He looked around at the guests. "Any questions? Oh, and one more thing. We need to know who is staying and who is going, so we can keep a head count and know who is where. How many are going?"

A bunch of hands went into the air. "OK, let me ask it another way. Is there anyone who is *not* going?"

"Lisa and I will stay here with Anya," Norma said.

"I think I'll take a shorter walk, maybe closer to camp," Lars said.

"All right. Everyone else is with me. Gather up there," he pointed, "under that cottonwood, in fifteen." He hopped off the bucket and gathered extra granola into his day pack.

CHAPTER 16

Tim set a steady pace, followed closely by the married couple, Millie and Darren. Carter filed in behind them and Ethan came last. He turned to glance at the camp as they left. Lisa's arms were folded tightly across her chest. Lars was rummaging through his gear.

Ethan had four snack bars in his pocket and swung his borrowed water bottle with the rhythm of his feet. He remembered coming down this trail the day before, but it looked quite different going up – the rocks seemed taller and the path wider. Though the cuts were still stiff on his skin, it felt good to be in motion again.

They walked in the center of the arroyo, where it was wide and flat. Ethan looked for the blue tent he'd seen yesterday and stopped for a moment to orient himself. Yes, that tent had been among those knee-high bushes toward the water. Their owners must have moved on, maybe while he and his adopted group were eating breakfast.

The trail abandoned the arroyo where it became cluttered with large rocks. He could see only Carter but could hear the rest of them scuffling ahead. The path rose steeply up an embankment, then twisted around jumbles of mahogany-colored sandstone. After about a half an hour, the group spread out and stopped to rest at the top of a rise. Carter sat close to Ethan and tucked his straight black hair behind his ears. His eyes were smoky and wide across the bridge of his nose.

"Ethan, right?"

Ethan nodded.

"Hey, did you see the stars last night, man? I thought I was James Tiberius Kirk, man. 'Third star on the right and straight on 'till morning'."

"I thought that was from Peter Pan."

Carter looked confused. "No, man. Star Trek."

"Well, sure, I meant..." Ethan shrugged and smiled.

"I just lay in the sand and watched the stars spin around. You can really notice it out here cause of these cliffs. If you find one close to the edge of a cliff, and stare at it, you can actually see it move away from the cliff, or behind it, and disappear. Really out of this world, man."

"Yes it is. Where you from, Carter?"

"Seattle."

"Really? You a student? Or have a line of work?"

"University of Washington, first year. General studies right now but I'm working to narrow it down. I never thought about it before this trip, but astronomy might be a very cool thing. That or horticulture." He looked over to Ethan. "What about you?"

"Just finished under-grad, sociology, with a minor in pre-law. Bloomington, Illinois. Decided to party in Moab for a couple of weeks, check out the night scene, learn how to mountain bike. You can see what that got me." He grinned and pointed to the fresh scabs on his legs.

"Oh, wow. Hey, does pre-law make you like law enforcement? An officer of the court and all that?" Carter scrunched his nose.

"No, not law enforcement."

Carter gave Ethan a sly grin.

"You won't like, go to jail if you party down a little?"

"No," Ethan said tentatively.

"Cool, man. Forget a party in Moab. You and me'll have a quick toke tonight, light up, and kick back. My pal Alan was supposed to be with me on this trip but he got the flu really bad the day before we were supposed to meet up." He leaned toward Ethan. "So, I got plenty of stash and nobody to smoke it with," he whispered. "Home grown."

"Cool," Ethan said, though he wasn't quite sure. He'd smoked some pot in college the previous year, at a couple of parties, chasing a cute skirt, but nothing since then. Dope convictions did not look good on grad school entrance applications. Pot was still not legal in his state.

Tim stood and waved for them to resume their hike. Ethan waited until everyone else had begun working their way up the trail. He stood and gazed across the landscape. Blue sky peeked through a narrow arch high on the southern rim, maybe eight hundred feet above him and some distance up the trail.

"Hey," he said, pointing toward the arch. Then he realized no one had heard him. He smiled and regained his rhythm, following the sound of voices.

CHAPTER 17

About an hour later, the group stopped at a level spot for a drink of water. Ethan turned and looked down the trail, where he recognized a patch of prickly pear he'd passed through coming up. He could no longer see the river or the grove of cottonwoods where they were camped. Tim announced they were closing in on the old still and motioned them along.

"It's like another planet, isn't it?" Carter turned toward him. Ethan's mind flashed for a moment to his off-campus dungeon, curtains drawn shut by his roommate for another marathon video game tournament, Ethan memorizing material for final exams.

"Yes, it is. And I bet it's really different from Seattle."

"No shit. I've never seen sky so blue or rocks so red."

"For sure."

"Or so many rocks at all."

Carter turned back to the trail and they labored up in silence. The path curved between large boulders then rose at a more gentle slope along a rounded hill that seemed to be made of one huge rock. Though he had his general bearings, the view going up the path was very different from the view going down. Ethan felt along the smooth stone on his left to a spot where the trail curved to the right. There, just inches from his face, a small, stone-etched warrior leapt into view. Startled, he stepped back and stared at it. It was the petroglyph that marked the way across the dome, leading to the northern drainage, the one Relic had drawn for him. Though mostly hidden by sage, he'd found it on his way down to the river the day before. He looked more closely at it this time.

A circle-shaped shield, pecked into the stone, hid most of the warrior's body. His rounded head wore a pair of curved lines on top, maybe some sort of headgear. His legs stood straight below the shield. One arm reached out with a spear in hand. This man had once walked and defended the plateau above, Ethan realized. Now, the man walked on the legs of history.

Carter trudged ahead, eyes on the ground. No one had seen the small guidepost but Ethan.

Something about the stylized warrior drew his eyes upward again, toward the passage to higher ground. He realized the spear held by the warrior pointed to a fold in the rock that led gently higher and away from the path. The petroglyph was showing him a way forward. How could he resist? He could always turn back if he needed to… He hesitated, then walked up the trail and called to Carter.

"Yeah?" Carter turned.

"Hey, Carter, I think I'm going to go on back down to camp. I'm still pretty tired from the other day. This uphill stuff is getting to be too much."

"Really?" He glanced farther up the path. "I don't think it's far now."

"Yeah, but I've seen it, remember? I came down this way, after I fell."

"Oh, yeah, well, sure, man."

"Tell Tim for me, will you, when you all get to the still. Just tell him I'll meet you all back at camp. No worries."

Carter seemed to think about it for a moment. "I think he wants us to stay together, but hey man, whatever you want to do."

"Thanks, Carter. I'll be fine. See you all back at camp."

"Will do." He waved at Ethan and turned back to the trail.

Ethan walked slowly back toward the partially concealed petroglyph and glanced behind him to make sure Carter was still hiking away. His heart beat quickened. He turned and hopped up the narrow passage that led to the top of the red rock dome.

CHAPTER 18

Ethan labored up a steep, slick portion of rock and reached a level area where he walked for a while and caught his breath. Looking back, he could not see the main trail and heard not a sound from the others. These canyons volleyed some noises back and forth, for all to hear, yet muffled others entirely. When the breeze stopped, he heard no sound at all. He smiled at the silence, the freedom.

So far, the general direction he wanted to go had been pretty clear. He was now on the upper part of a huge rise separating the north canyon, in front of him, from the south, where he'd just left. He let his eyes wander over the ground, around the prickly cactus, delicate grasses and car-sized boulders. A natural pathway presented itself on his right, winding through a jumble of knee-high rocks.

He picked his way over the uneven surface and

onto a more open course. Though not well-worn like a trail, it seemed to have been partially cleared. Rocks had been stacked on each other three or four high on either side at random intervals, like stone age cairns. He continued on for another quarter mile or so, staring at the russet-colored cliffs on the far side of the high, northern canyon.

He stopped and took a long drink from his half-empty bottle. Better go easy on the rest of it.

He came to a huge stone on his right, a pebble set by a giant, and patted its rough surface. In the distance to his left, he could see a triangle of green - maybe the trees by the camp. He walked slowly around the stone, watching its surface as he went, when an unusual form slid into view: a single, anthropomorphic petroglyph. Its body was triangular, with stick arms and legs attached. Antlers, like those of a deer, sprouted from its head and large, round balls hung like earrings from its skull. In its right hand, it pointed a staff with perpendicular hash marks along the top. The strange staff-man faced the twin canyons directly toward the river.

He examined the pock marks that gave the art its shape and texture, and imagined the hands that made it. He looked again in the direction where the staff-man stared. A sliver of river shone in the distance. He stepped four feet left and four feet right of the petroglyph. On either side, the river disappeared from view.

What he wouldn't give for a camera about now. To the north, the red canyon rim rose several hundred feet above the plateau where he stood. To the south, the canyon was far more distant, blurred by the haze of late afternoon sun. To the west, the canyons came toward each other on this side of the river, like two hands reaching to grasp. Across the water, the high rim could have tricked him into thinking it was all one single massive wall of rock. If he hadn't known the river was there, or seen it where the staff-man pointed, he would never have known it existed.

It suddenly occurred to him that he would never again live in the off-campus dungeon. There was simply nothing to pull him back there. Nothing. Good riddance, he thought, to the blackened, closet-sized bedroom and stacks of course books, the squat little table lamp, and the incessant bleating of his roommate's latest video game. He smiled and took a long, deep breath.

The heat of the sun began baking his arms and neck. He moved around what he'd named the Giant's Pebble and found a shady spot. A cut on his right leg had begun to weep some fluid and his muscles ached. He sat in the sand for a short rest, and dozed.

CHAPTER 19

Norma sat quietly enjoying the sound of the river as it tossed itself over rocks near the shore and through the branches of a fallen tree. Tall cottonwoods kept her cool in the shade. She slid her shoes off and dug her toes into the sand.

Her niece seemed restless and bored. She sat on the edge of a raft, touching and shaking the dead electronic gizmo. She looked up, found a camp chair, and carried it over to Norma.

"It's much cooler here, Lisa." Norma pointed next to her. Lisa unfolded the chair, adjusted it in the sand and sat.

"Still not working?" Norma pointed to the iPod.

"No, Aunt Norma, it's completely broken. I tried drying it out, shaking it, pushing the on and off button. Nothing works."

"You can get a new one when we get home."

Lisa wrinkled her nose. "I won't have any music for the rest of the trip."

"That's not true at all, dear. I've been listening to Peter, Paul and Mary all afternoon," Norma smiled.

Lisa looked at her sideways, a skeptic.

"If you keep your favorite music in your head, you can listen anytime you like."

Lisa shifted in her chair and stared at the sand for a moment. "Who's Peter and Mary?"

"Peter, Paul and Mary. I'm listening to their song, 'Blowing in the Wind.'"

"What's it sound like?"

"It's called folk music, something you can play on just a guitar or even just with the sound of your voice. Very nice music for a spot like this. Want to hear some of it?"

"Sure."

"I'm no singer," she chuckled, "but I'll try." She cleared her throat. "My favorite part is 'How many times must a man look up, before he can see the sky? How many ears must one man have before he can hear people cry? The answer my friend, is blowing in the wind, the answer is blowing in the wind'."

Lisa glanced at Norma, then out to the river, and

let out a nervous laugh.

"I warned you, I can't carry a tune in a bucket."

"That's silly, Aunt Norma."

"Silly," she sat straighter and smiled, "but true."

"It sounded nice to me." Lisa shrugged and returned the smile.

Sounds of chatter reached the beach as members of the group returned from their hike to the old still.

Darren and his wife, Millie, shuffled into Norma's view and Lisa waved at them.

Darren waved back briskly and pivoted away toward their tent, which they had pitched nearly eighty yards away from the others.

Norma shook her head and turned back to Lisa. "Now, where were we?"

CHAPTER 20

Ethan awoke with a start, kicking the dirt at his feet. His eyes searched the area quickly. Then he rose carefully with his back to the tall stone and listened. Nothing. He circled the Giant's Pebble one step at a time, but there was no one there. He scanned the rough terrain but saw no movement, no swirling dust, no shadows out of place. Still, he could not shake the thought that he was, or had been, watched.

The sun continued to slide toward the northwestern wall and he decided he could dally no more. Whatever spooked him out of slumber also hurried his feet along a narrow game trail toward the northern arroyo.

The plateau dipped steadily down toward the narrow north canyon. In some spots he lost all signs of the trail, but deer prints eventually led him in a steep switchback pattern. He stopped and sat at a large, bread-shaped boulder and looked up the north canyon to his right. The drainage petered out among a jumble of large rocks at the base of high, sunburnt cliffs. At about his same elevation, across the way, a burst of green moss and ferns clung to the canyon wall. He recognized it as another spring, like the one Relic used for his gin-making still. He could refill his water bottle there, but the distance was discouraging. It would be easier for him to go on down the canyon to camp.

He scanned the area, looking for interesting rocks and outcrops across from him. A bend in the seasonal stream curved perfectly flat in a crescent-moon, several feet higher than the main drainage. He sat up. Lower down, a set of two dark squares caught his attention. From this distance, they looked like dark square boxes. He knew that what seemed to rise up from the dirt could actually be receding into it. Were they holes?

Something to his right, above the squares, pulled his eyes in that direction then disappeared. To his far left, he heard the sound of boots on hard scrabble coming up the arroyo toward the holes. He watched a man come slowly up the trail, then place his hands on his knees, catching his breath. The sounds of his feet disappeared as he crossed a sandy patch and wandered aimlessly, looking up and down the canyon walls. Suddenly, Ethan recognized Lars; his generous stomach, his slightly swaying gait, his brightly colored shirt. He smiled and thought about the distance between them. No real point in yelling, but if he moved quickly, he might meet up with Lars before he turned back to camp.

Lars turned and ambled out of view.

Ethan started down across the rocky incline, making his own switchback pattern. The game trail had disappeared. After a bit, he came to an outcrop and went to the top to look around.

He heard a woman's voice yelling something. Sounds in the tight canyon bounced off the walls, making it hard to tell where it was coming from. After a few minutes, he saw motion in the area he'd seen Lars. The sway of her hips gave her away – Anya was hiking up the steep arroyo, calling for Lars.

Something else caught his eye then backed out of sight.

Anya seemed to notice the square holes, so out of place here, and moved closer to them. Ethan stood and stretched, and looked for a better path down into the arroyo. He began to pick his way across the rocks then stopped to look again. Anya was standing at the square hole, staring in, when someone dashed from behind a rock. A man raised a shovel high in the air, rushed her from behind, and swung.

Ethan could not believe what he saw. The man's shovel hit her head from behind and slammed her to the ground. A second after he saw it, the sickening sound reached his ears. The man with the shovel ran back behind the rocks, out of view again. Ethan didn't know whether to scream, run down the trail, or stay where he stood.

Anya lay there, three or four hundred yards away, still as a corpse.

CHAPTER 21

Shock gripped his muscles and froze the air in his lungs. "Holy shit," he muttered.

He scanned the north canyon then looked again at Anya. No one and no thing was moving. Whoever had attacked her was in hiding, or had left on a path beyond Ethan's view. He had to do something, right now.

He had no weapon, but, then, the attacker had only used a shovel. Maybe the shovel was all he had. Ethan searched the ground quickly for hand-sized rocks, putting two into his pockets and keeping one in each palm. He began to make his way along more of the deer tracks. After several steps, he stopped to look and listen, but the area was silent as a ghost. Rocks in the arroyo rolled narrow shadows across the hard dirt.

He made his way down a steep incline until the ground began to level out near a smooth, half-buried boulder. He stepped around the base, watching for any kind of movement as he rounded the corner. Artwork in the rock stopped him short. An etched warrior met him at eye-level, a twin to the one that marked the way on the other side of the small plateau. It had the same circle-shaped shield pecked into the stone, the same curved lines on top of the warrior's head. It marked the other end of the access trail over the plateau.

He took a few deep breaths and steadied his feet.

The absence of human sound encouraged him to move faster. Whoever had attacked Anya must have moved out by now. He realized that the flat, crescent shaped area he'd noticed from the plateau was now slightly above him. He was close. His grip tightened on the fist-sized rocks and he walked briskly across the level part of the drainage.

After a dozen long strides he could see Anya, a limp bundle of arms and legs in the sand. He forgot his fear and ran to her, dropping the stones from his fingers.

"Oh, Christ." Her hair was tangled in a woven mess. "Anya." He said softly. He began to shake, nearly out of control. He willed his hands to touch her shoulders. She was warm. He moved his knees close to her back and rolled her gently face up. He wanted to speak, to shout out her name, to call for help, but he simply could not. His breath came only in short, forced gasps. Slowly, he moved the hair from her closed eyes and watched her face for any kind of motion, any sign whether she was alive or dead.

Time twisted like a dark tornado, suspended in one horrible moment before her mouth opened and she inhaled.

"Beth," he whispered, then realized his mistake. His shoulders shook and he wept openly until the surge was exhausted.

Slowly, he began to feel the sand in his shoes and a coolness in the air. He began to breathe evenly again.

Anya's chest rose and fell in smooth rhythm, but her eyes remained closed and her muscles limp.

"Anya," Ethan shook her gently but got no response. Then, a hard sound, the echo of boots on gravel, rose up the canyon.

Someone was moving toward them.

CHAPTER 22

He knew he didn't have much time. He reached for her wrist and felt a slow, strong pulse. He gently lifted her eyelids and checked her pupils. They both seemed to match each other, which he knew was a good sign, but he wasn't sure if they were more dilated than normal. The hair on the back of her head was matted with dark, sticky blood.

Ethan moved behind Anya and reached under her shoulders. He pulled her several feet across the sand, closer toward a truck-size boulder. The dead weight was heavier than he'd expected and he was soon panting under the strain. He stopped to listen again and heard the distant kick of a rock. He braced himself and dragged Anya to the shade of the smooth sandstone and laid her head down gently.

A pair of crows circled above, gossiping in their

own language, their caws echoing quickly against the high walls. It was hard to tell which sounds were original and which were repeats.

The canyon slowly filled with silence and Ethan kept his eyes on Anya. His hands dug nervously through loose gravel that gathered by the rock and he thought about hiding her under the sand, like a tourist buried neck-deep in the ocean beach, then promptly rejected it. He had neither the shovel nor the time to do it. A flat, round object reached his fingers as he sifted, but it was not a stream-worn stone. He glanced at it. It was coated in dirt, but seemed to have a distinct pattern with an uneven hole in the middle. He rubbed it with his thumb until it became shiny. Odd. It must be a large button from someone's clothes, or maybe a latch from a day-pack. Trash. He remembered the ethos, "pack it in, pack it out." He tucked it into his pocket.

The crows had gone home for the evening as shadows enveloped the canyon. He strained to hear anything human, but was disappointed. He watched Anya for a while longer. She seemed to breathe more comfortably, almost like she was sleeping. The shade was welcome relief from the sun, but he remembered how quickly the night became cold. They needed a way to stay warm. He licked his lips. They would also soon be out of water. He needed to get back down to camp for help.

Suddenly, boots were scraping again, this time across the rough limestone bed of the arroyo, and they were close.

He remembered the rocks in his pockets and grabbed them, then moved around the large rock and downslope of it. A tall figure passed quickly through his peripheral vision. Ethan steeled his nerves and moved to intercept him. Ethan could hear each step now, even the labored breathing of the man coming his way. He hid behind a waist high rock and prepared himself.

CHAPTER 23

"Anya!" the man shouted. The sudden sound jarred Ethan like a slap on the jaw and his teeth clenched. Then, he realized the voice was Tim's. He was searching the drainage. Ethan released his breath and let his arms hang loose. Of course. Tim and the group had made it back to camp and discovered Anya was missing.

"Tim!" Ethan stood from behind the low rock and waved. Tim stopped in his tracks and turned. A look of shock, and perhaps displeasure, crossed his face in an instant but was quickly replaced with a wide smile.

"Ethan, where have you been? We expected to see you back at camp. We thought the smell of supper would…"

"Tim, stop. Anya's been hurt."

"Anya is with you?"

"She was attacked. Someone hit her with a shovel and she went down. I found her and pulled her into the shade."

Tim's face tensed for a moment. "Where is she? Show me," he demanded.

Ethan waved him forward and they hurried to the shadow of the large rock. Anya had not moved.

"Oh, shit." Tim went quickly to her, checked her pulse and felt her forehead. Like Ethan had done, he lifted each eyelid and checked her pupils.

"What happened, again?"

"Someone hit her with a shovel, from behind."

Tim looked at Ethan with a hint of disbelief. "Who would do such a thing?"

"Hell if I know, Tim. I was farther up the canyon," he waved toward the plateau, "and saw it happen. I could hardly believe it. Whoever hit her is gone. I couldn't tell from that distance who it was. I just saw it happen, then I heard it, but the attacker disappeared."

"OK, OK," Tim said, turning back to Anya. "I think she's got a concussion, to be knocked out like this."

"We've got to keep her warm," Ethan said. "But there's someone out there, someone dangerous. Why the hell would he hit her like that?"

"You're right, it's going to get cold tonight. We've got to keep her warm and watch her, but I don't think we should move her."

"It would be tough to do, anyway. I moved her a few feet, to the shelter here, and it wore me out. Camp's a long ways down the canyon."

"Right." Tim sat back on his haunches and watched Anya thoughtfully. "I've got a whole group of inexperienced rafters down there too. Someone's got to stay with them."

"Especially with some crazy guy wandering around."

"No shit. There's a thousand places to hide around here. We don't know who he is or what he wants. I've got no choice but to stay with the group, and watch them tonight."

Ethan put his hands in his pockets. "I should stay here."

"Yes, I agree." Tim looked at him. "I could send someone else to stay with you over night, but none of them are experienced hikers."

Ethan shifted the weight on his feet.

"Besides, it'll be dark in less than an hour. It's not likely whoever did this would be running around after nightfall," Tim rubbed his forehead. "Too many ways to twist an ankle or fall. It's too dangerous."

Spare me the false encouragement, Ethan thought. "Anyway, if whoever did this is still here, you'd just be sending someone else into harm's way."

Tim nodded. "I'll run back down to camp and get you sleeping bags and water for tonight. And something to eat." He thought for a moment. "Then, I can come back up again at first light to see if we can get her back to camp."

"Sure." Ethan etched the sand with his foot, running the memory through his mind again. He knew he'd also have to stay awake and watch over Anya through the night.

"All right. I'll be back as soon as I can. Keep a close eye on her."

"What about getting her help? I mean, tomorrow."

"Let's see how she is in the morning. If she's still unconscious, I'll have to run the rapids out of here by myself and get help. If she's better, we can at least move her to camp and stay another day or two if she needs it."

"Her safety comes first, above all else," Ethan said with more authority than he expected.

"You are right about that, my friend. I better get going." Tim stood and jogged quickly away. Every few seconds, he could hear Tim's boots on the rocky trail, growing ever quieter.

CHAPTER 24

Clang! Clang! Clang! Tim banged a ladle against the soup pot. "Everyone, I need your attention!"

The married couple, Darren and Millie, were already nearby, seated on the river bank. They turned to listen. Lisa and her aunt Norma looked up from their conversation and smiled. Carter strolled closer to the group.

Tim turned one of the camp buckets upside down and stood on top of it. "Where's Lars, does anyone know?"

"Latrine, I think," Carter pointed to the trail that led to the baño, beyond the sights and sounds of camp.

"OK. Listen, I have some unfortunate news. Anya has fallen and hurt herself, up the canyon a ways. She was looking for Ethan, I guess, who, well, he actually found her first. Anyway, she'll be all right," he said hopefully. "But, she's out of commission for the time being."

"She's all right, though?" Norma asked. Lisa leaned

forward in her chair and clasped her hands together.

"Yes, but we'll have to see tomorrow if she can make it back down the canyon to join us. If not…" Tim paused. "Well, we'll go on without her, if we have to, and ask the park service to bring her back."

"How did she get hurt?" Norma asked.

"She fell and may have sprained an ankle," he lied smoothly, wanting the group to stay calm. "She looks a little bruised up. She was probably just going too fast, looking up and down the canyon instead of where she was going." He shrugged. "It can happen on these rough trails. But we train for this kind of thing all the time."

"What are we going to do now?" Carter rubbed his hands on his hips, like he was scratching them.

"I'm going to bring them sleeping bags, food, and water, then be right back down to camp. We have chicken parmesan for you for dinner. With Anya temporarily out of commission, I'll ask for some help with the kitchen chores. If everyone pitches in, it'll be a cinch."

"Of course we'll help any way we can," Norma volunteered.

"Tell Lars what's happened, when he's done at the baño. Meanwhile, Norma, I'll get the stove set up and leave you to cook the chicken."

"I used to cook for seven all the time. I think I can

still remember how it's done," Norma stood.

"I know you're all tired after the long hike today and we may have to break camp early in the morning. You should eat, clean up a bit, and call it a night. Get some good rest," Tim said.

"Wait, what if she can't come back down tomorrow? Who will row her raft?" Carter pointed at the boat.

"We'll figure it out tomorrow. I think she'll be just fine, maybe a little sore. One of you folks could handle a raft on the flat water, if Anya's not able to. And I can always run the rapids one raft at a time, then walk back upriver and run the second one through."

Carter seemed to think it over, his eyes on the ground. He mumbled something the others could not quite hear.

Tim smiled broadly and looked around at them. "You folks are the greatest. Anya and I really appreciate it, and I promise we won't give you any more excitement than exactly what you signed on for. This is your vacation, after all."

He stepped off his makeshift pedestal and began to rummage through the equipment.

CHAPTER 25

The longer Ethan thought about it, the more disturbing it became. There was simply no reason for anyone to attack someone in this canyon. Yet here Anya was, limp in the sand. He felt as helpless as she was.

He squeezed his hands inside his pockets to warm them and felt the odd button. He took it out and rubbed it aimlessly between his thumb and fingers. The rock they were near offered some shelter and would offer shade for tomorrow's heat. But it left them exposed on three sides and at risk from behind. If the attacker returned, he could get pretty close before Ethan would see him. Maybe he would hear him sooner than that, maybe not. Anya was exceptionally vulnerable in this spot.

He stood and moved away from her several hundred feet, walking a semi-circle around the large rock. Above, he could see a shelf of sorts in the limestone and ribs of horizontal sandstone above that. The limestone would hide their tracks up there. Maybe Tim would help him move Anya when he got back.

He realized he'd been rubbing the button hard, feeling unusual ridges and lines all across it. He looked more closely at it this time. The object was a nearly perfect circle with an uneven shaped hole in the center. On its surface were etched drawings, a little like the shape of northwestern Indian art, like renditions of a whale. No, not a whale. More like a dragon with a headdress. And the more he rubbed, the shinier it became. He held it up and saw the unmistakable shimmer of gold.

"What the hell?"

"Ethan!" Tim yelled from below. "I'm on my way up."

Ethan stared at the golden button a moment longer then dropped it in his pocket. He hustled past Anya and around the corner.

Tim hurried up the draw, sweat running down his face and arms. He'd run most of the way back. He carried two sleeping bags and shouldered a day pack.

"Here," Ethan said, trotting down to help. He grabbed the bags and together they climbed back up to Anya.

Tim sat in the sand and caught his breath.

He slipped the pack off his shoulders and tossed it at Ethan. "Two water bottles and trail snacks. Should hold you over."

"Thank you, Tim. Really." He set the sleeping bags in the sand. "If Anya wakes up, I'll get her as much water as she can handle."

"Yes. But be ready in case she throws up. Nausea can be a side effect of a concussion."

Anya stirred, just a bit. They watched for more movement, but she lay still again. The sky reddened along the canyon rim.

"Oh, and a flashlight too," Tim pointed to the daypack.

"Good thinking."

They sat in silence for a few moments.

"I told the group that Anya was hurt up here, but not that someone attacked her," Tim raised an open palm. "I was unsure whether to tell them that, but I'll watch over them all night, to be safe, and come back in the morning."

"Is there anyone with us who could have hurt her?" Ethan asked.

Tim held his breath a moment and looked up at Ethan. "Not that I know of, not likely a member of our group."

The implication was subtle, but it still turned Ethan's face red. "Hey, I never even met anyone in your group until a couple days ago. Why on earth would I want to see any of you hurt?"

"Calm down, I'm sorry." Tim held up his hands. "I'm really exhausted and worried. I shouldn't have said it that way, I didn't really mean anything. Of course you would have no reason to hurt Anya."

"Damn right."

"Why would I leave you with her if I thought you were the one who hurt her?"

Well, yes, that's right, Ethan thought. He nodded, compelled to take the apology.

A cool breeze brushed the sand at their feet and wove its way farther down the canyon. They sat for a moment, absorbed in their own thoughts.

Ethan felt the gold button again in his pocket. Maybe it wasn't trash, at least not modern trash. Frustration faded as astonishment took its place. The square holes. Someone is digging for something. And he may have found that very something.

"Tim!" he straightened his back. "Holy shit, I know what it is. Here, check this out." He handed the button to Tim. "It looks like an artifact of some kind."

Tim's face went white as he examined the object.

"This might be gold. Very old. It's no ordinary artifact," he said excitedly, then leveled his voice. "Well, maybe it is, maybe not. Where did you find this?"

"Right here." He pointed to the truck-sized rock above them. "In the sand at the base of it, here."

"Exactly there?"

"Yes. And, Tim," Ethan added, "there are square shaped holes in the ground about a hundred yards that way," he pointed to the northeast. "I saw them when Anya was attacked. She was coming toward them when the guy hit her with a shovel. Maybe this is some kind of archeological dig!"

"No way would he get a permit. This guy has something serious he wants kept quiet." Tim rubbed the button and went deep into his own thoughts. "This is no big deal," he said about the button, "but maybe it's what he's looking for. We have to report any looting of artifacts we find. It's part of our license requirements for guiding groups through the canyons. I'll take it back to the boats."

"Wait. What if the looter comes back here? I could use that to bargain with him if I had to." Ethan reached for the button. "Just in case." Tim stared at the artifact as Ethan took it from his open hand.

"Don't be stupid, Ethan! If he'll hit Anya with a

shovel just for looking at his dig, he'll kill both of you for taking a piece of his loot. He's not going to bargain with you."

Ethan's face flushed. "I'll threaten to throw it where he'll never find it."

"That's just as crazy. Damn it, Ethan, that thing is evidence, too," Tim said, reaching out.

"Just the same, I'm going to hang onto it. I'll only give it up if I have to." Ethan tucked the button deep into his pants pocket and stared at Tim defiantly.

Tim put his arm back down, mildly annoyed, but working to suppress it. "It's no bargaining chip, Ethan. At least promise me you'll keep it hidden from him."

Ethan nodded and they sat silently for a moment.

"OK," Tim sighed, "I'd better get back before it's fully dark. I'll come back in the morning. Take good care of Anya for us, okay?"

"Of course." Ethan's lips tightened as he looked over at her. Evening colors were bleeding away in the dark - he would need the flashlight soon.

Tim stood and moved quickly past the rock and out of sight. After several minutes, Ethan could hear the sound of footsteps moving further down the canyon and away from him and Anya.

He felt the ancient button through his pants leg.

Something bothered Ethan just beyond his conscious thought, some piece of a puzzle jammed into place; close to the right fit, but not quite.

****

On a ledge a little higher up the canyon, a pair of eyes watched patiently.

CHAPTER 26

"Damn," he scolded himself. He'd let Tim draw them into an argument and forgot to ask for his help moving Anya to safer ground. Better get going before it's too dark. He walked quickly around several small boulders upslope and found his way to an upper ledge made of limestone, where the wind kept the sand from accumulating. Above that were several horizontal layers of sandstone - not caves exactly, but with deep recesses that would protect them from wind or rain, and also might help them hide. It would be no easy task to get Anya up here, but he had to try.

He went back and examined her again. She seemed to be sleeping peacefully, but he knew she could be seriously injured. He gathered his resolve, hooked his arms under hers, and lifted her three quarters of the way off the ground. Then, he began to walk backward, dragging her feet behind them.

He stopped several times before reaching the limestone lip then went slowly along the ledge and upwards to a good foothold. He stopped again to catch his breath and look around. He was most of the way there. Dragging her across the rock was trickier than across the sand, but a little faster. Eventually, he rested with Anya at the base of the sandstone recesses. He twisted his head, looking for the best one. Unfortunately, it looked like the farthest one from him was the deepest, the most sheltered.

He took several full breaths and pulled Anya up to the first sandstone lip, then dragged her diagonally to the next level.

"What the hell am I doing?" he asked himself. Sweat drenched his arms and legs. "Can't stop now," he answered his own thoughts.

The last level was the hardest. Ethan could not release Anya or she would roll and fall back down to the limestone. But he could not get a solid grip with his feet on the slick rock, either. He leaned back against the stone and crabbed his way up and across, dragging Anya several inches at a time.

Finally, he reached the opening of the upper ledge, and pulling her became a little easier. When he had her well inside the overhang, he laid her gently on the sand

and sat back, panting.

The sky was nearly black and he could barely make out shapes in the arroyo beneath them. He slid off the rock and stumbled across loose rocks and small brush he'd been able to navigate on the way up. Luckily, the truck-sized boulder was still visible against the skyline, and he felt his way to the daypack and pulled out the flashlight.

The battery was weak but the light was more than enough to help him find the sleeping bags. He shouldered the pack and carried the bags back to the limestone ledge and tossed them up. Then he took off his shirt and went back to the large boulder. Flashlight aimed at his footprints, he swept his shirt all around, blending them into the sand, the way he'd seen Relic do it. When he reached the limestone, he knew the footprints would end and stopped sweeping the ground. He shook the dust from his shirt and put it back on. He hopped up the short rise, grabbed the bags and used the light to find his way back to Anya.

Inside the overhang, the light showed a deep recess. He rolled out the bags, unzipped one, and carefully laid it across Anya, tucking in the edges under her. He felt her forehead: no fever as far as he could tell. He rolled the hood of the bag into a pillow and angled it carefully beneath her head.

He lay there for several minutes, exhausted. He took a long drink from the water bottle and wished he'd had some of the home-made gin that character Relic had cooked up. He smiled at the thought. Then he wondered - what the hell was a guy like that doing in these canyons, really? Just moonshining?

And who was up here digging, if not someone from the rafting group? Maybe they were camped farther upriver, above where Anya's group was staying. Were they really looting Indian artifacts? Was there a black market for that?

He looked in the pack and found a pile of trail bars. Greedily, he tore open one, then another, and ate them as fast as he could. He took several long drinks from the water bottle then set it back in the pack. He left one bottle for Anya untouched. He unrolled the other sleeping bag and slid inside, his muscles aching even with that small effort. He looked around one more time, assuring himself they weren't sleeping in a rattlesnake nest, then turned off the flashlight.

Damn it, he wished Anya would wake up.

Stars dotted the night sky outside his narrow hideaway. Embarrassed at himself, he remembered his first reaction to finding Anya, and his memory of another he'd cared for and lost. What had Relic said? We are all spirits, having a human experience. But some kind of human evil was out there, stealing artifacts and threatening his new friends. He suddenly thought of Anya exactly that way, as a dear friend to be protected. He burrowed deeper into the bag.

Exhaustion overtook him and he joined Anya in a distant, troubled, slumber.

CHAPTER 27

Bobby couldn't rest.

Harold and Trevor snored like lumberjacks. Bobby moved away and onto rocks above their camp, listening to the sounds of the night: soft rustlings and scratches by deer in the trees and maybe a coyote in the grass. After supper and a couple of beers, they'd talked him out of going back up to the dig tonight. He took the pistol from his shoulder harness and rolled the cylinder. He loved the feel of it in his hands, especially when he was shooting. Harold teased him about the shoulder harness the way an older brother might, but Bobby knew it was a really nice touch. It ought to impress Boss, his uncle. It was unique, and Bobby was fast on the draw. Someday, Bobby was going to ride that wave, up on top, just like Boss. Maybe even higher. Someday soon.

But this current trouble was a puzzle. What were

people from the rafting group doing all the way up the small side canyon? These tourists usually stayed close to the trails and moved on through. He worried even more about locating the same place he'd found the Anasazi sandal last season. He was sure it was where they were digging, but, so far, they'd had no luck at all. Only a couple of broken arrowheads for all their effort. If they didn't hit something soon, they'd have to break off and try another spot later. Boss would not be happy. That sandal must've brought a pretty penny.

He needed a walk, even in the dark. Star-light lent some sense of shape to the objects near at hand, so he stood and walked slowly along a flat ledge toward the trail to the old moonshine camp. After a while, he realized he was on the trail itself, and kept going up just to stretch his legs and keep warm in the cool night air. He rounded a bend in the trail, worked up a short set of switchbacks, then leveled out and looked back toward the river. That's when he heard it: two loud pops in quick order, down below.

Shit. It had to be a small pistol, maybe from camp. Had Harold woken up and shot at something?

Bobby ran back down the trail as quickly as he dared. Suddenly, he tripped forward and shielded his face just as he hit the ground.

"Shit, shit, shit," he swore to himself. He stood and brushed himself off. As anxious as he was, he had to slow down. He shuffled farther across the flats, then down the short switchbacks to a spot above the camp. He peered over a large rock but could not see any movement and heard no more sounds.

He scrambled farther down the trail, then across the brush into camp. He stood there for a moment, panting and confused. A fingernail moon had risen, pitching its veneer of light across the ground and everything looked all right. Harold and Trevor were in their sleeping bags by the back wall of sandstone. Their gear was where they'd left it.

But something was wrong. No one made a sound. No one was snoring.

He looked nervously about and pulled his pistol from the holster. He walked slowly over to Harold.

"Hey, Harold. Buddy," he whispered, moving closer. "Wake up, man, I think I heard some shots." He came to the sleeping bag and shook it hard. Harold's head rolled back and forth and his face stared upwards, a small red hole in the middle of his forehead.

"Holy mother," Bobby exclaimed, stumbling backward. He looked toward Trevor and knew he was shot, too. Who the hell did this?

Bobby's head swung back and forth, his eyes straining into the night. He went to the gear by the shovels and found a large flashlight but kept it turned off. He held his pistol out in front of him and began to trot away from camp, out across the flats and up the north side canyon, up toward their dig. Whoever did this was going to die.

CHAPTER 28

The sound of rock rolling against rock echoed into his sandstone sanctuary and woke him from a dead sleep. Ethan's eyes were wide but saw nothing but black space between him and the overhang. He waited and checked himself. Yes, he'd heard it, and it came from close at hand, below the ledge.

He strained his ears and heard another sound, lower but still unmistakable. The sound of boots on rock.

He turned and squirmed quietly from his sleeping bag. He put the flashlight in his pants pocket, afraid to turn it on lest he give himself away, rolled gently to the edge of their sandstone shelter, and listened again.

A harsh light shone across the arroyo, about a hundred yards away, then switched off. If it were Tim again, he'd be calling out to them. Whoever it was used the light to move forward, then waited and lit the area again, repeating the process. It allowed him to move up across the rugged terrain but also broadcast his location and where he was headed. Fortunately, it must mean his night vision was not very good. Unfortunately, he was headed in their direction.

Recalling what mother birds do for their young, Ethan found his plan. He might need to find water on the run so he grabbed the filter-bottle Relic had given him. He rolled farther toward and over the gentle edge of the sandstone and put his feet on the ledge below it. He could hear the intruder moving closer. Ethan sat and slid as quietly as he could down to the next level, then the next, to the bed of limestone where eons of spring run-off had rounded its sharp features.

The flashlight suddenly lit the ground fifty feet to the right of him, then turned off. He had to move now, before the intruder closed in and used the light again. And, contrary to all of his instincts, he had to make some noise.

Ethan took a deep breath. He knelt to the ground and found a small rock, which he tossed down the arroyo. The light flashed on, searching below him. Then Ethan made his way up the dry creek bed, making plenty of noise as he went.

The intruder seemed to be confused, moving his light away from Ethan, then swinging it back wildly toward him, then away again. Finally, he seemed to realize Ethan was moving up the canyon, not down it. He'd gained a few precious moments with the distraction.

The intruder began moving methodically up the sandy bed and over to the limestone. At the lip, he moved onto the flat surface and began to run, lighting the way as he went. He was no longer turning the flashlight off.

Ethan saw the intruder rush past the spot where Anya was hidden, and breathed a quick sigh of relief. But when the light searched ever higher, and ever closer, he panicked. Without thought of injury, he tore across the limestone formation and back onto sandy soil, running over and into rocks and brush, spinning past the ones he hit, holding his arms in front of him like a blind man down a gauntlet.

The intruder picked up his pace, no doubt hearing Ethan's reckless moves, seeing where to place his own steps to avoid the hazards Ethan was tripping into.

Ethan's pounding heart throbbed in his ears. With his every step, the light moved markedly closer. The faster he tried to run, the worse it seemed and he knew the light would soon overtake him. Ethan's hands slapped a large boulder on his left and he spun to get around it. On the other side, he saw the light slip past and above him, searching. He could hear the man's raspy breath as he labored at a near run up the drainage. Ethan felt the stone behind him and shuffled along the edge.

The intruder stopped just within Ethan's line of sight, waving the light before him, examining ahead and also on the ground. Footprints. He would see Ethan's footprints.

Ethan felt the rock drop away as he reached the end of it, and then spun around it. In that second, the light blasted where he'd been, but he was hidden. The intruder stood still for a moment, catching his breath, then turned off the lantern.

Ethan's night vision returned quickly, and he could see some major shapes around him. To his left, along the edge of the canyon, he thought he could see a way to higher ground. He took a deep breath then moved as fast as he could, past the intruder's line of sight and between a pair of fin-shaped rocks. Ethan stopped to listen. The man lit the area where Ethan had just passed through.

A shot rang out like thunder and the sound bounced off the sandstone walls like a rubber ball. Ethan's body tensed, then began to shake. The shot went where he'd just crossed to the fins. The sonofabitch had a pistol and was using it.

Ethan turned back into the fins and felt his way along the walls. Stones in the center of his path nearly tripped him. He kept moving, but the passage was narrowing, slowing his progress. A hint of light caught his peripheral vision and he hurried even faster into the tightening crevasse.

His heart felt like it would explode, his brain reduced to instinctual fear. Part of him thought he should stop and try to hide but he kept moving. Then, the passage narrowed to just inches apart. It may as well have been a locked, steel door.

CHAPTER 29

By the time he'd gotten back to camp, the kitchen had been cleaned up and the group all seemed to be snug in their tents. Only Carter slept under the stars. Tim leaned against one of the cottonwoods and took a deep breath. Then he heard a sharp sound, just barely, higher up the drainage. Was someone other than Anya and Ethan up there after all? Tim pulled his hat tighter on his head and pushed away from the tree.

He'd made more than one trip up and down this side canyon, and knew the best path to travel. A sliver of moon hung above the higher canyon wall and helped create a soft light on landmarks he could see along the way. He knew he could not sprint the mile or more to the truck-sized boulder where he'd left them, so he quickened his pace but kept it steady.

****

Millie woke in her tent from a nightmare - someone had been firing a gun at them. She and Darren had been fleeing through darkened streets, down a blind alley, to a curtain they could not open. She nudged at her husband until she realized his sleeping bag was empty. Her stomach dropped. Where could he be this time of night?

"Darren?" she whispered then strained to hear. Nothing. She laid back and stared at the inside of their tent, reminding herself they were hell and away from any city streets. She thought of their day in the raft, bobbing and turning in the river, the hot, clear sun warming their bones. Eventually, her breathing slowed. Darren could not have gone far. He must have been hungry, looking for a snack. Or gone to the secluded camp bathroom, many yards away. That had to be it. She would not even bother to ask him, she decided; they'd had enough stress lately, and he'd accuse her of clinging again. She just needed to give him some more space, so to speak. She closed her eyes and listened until, finally, she slid back into a restless slumber.

CHAPTER 30

So this is what it felt like right before you die. Ashes to ashes, dust to dust. Ethan stroked the stone face like the talisman he'd had as a child. He felt an odd sense of companionship, or maybe just a wishful alliance, with the invincible rock. The light found the entrance to the passage, flashing up and down the fins with a disorienting strobe. The intruder had found the pathway and was coming in.

Ethan shimmied farther into the narrows until his foot struck a rock four feet high near the pinched end of the fins. Wedging against the higher stone, he got his feet on the rock and stood up, feeling his way along. Balanced there, he stopped and watched the light snake its way closer and closer. Tightening walls bounced the glare between them, creating an eerie glow with sharp shadows. The intruder was backlit against the rocks. He seemed young and moved with the purpose of a zealot, a gleaming pistol waving like an extension of his hand.

Ethan's right arm swung backward, feeling for more rock, searching a way to go higher, but he found nothing but air. He turned. Sensing open space in front of him, he shuffled his feet to the edge of his perch. The fins parted up here and ended.

Light followed up the narrow path straight toward Ethan. Without thinking, he blinked his eyes and jumped.

CHAPTER 31

Another blast from the pistol reverberated up and down the canyon walls. Ethan found himself in the sand, his left shoulder burrowed in. He rolled, then squatted on the ground, watching behind him. Thin rays of flashlight escaped through cracks in the tall fins. The intruder had fired another shot, but Ethan had already fallen through the gap seven feet above the ground.

"Get back here, you creepy sonofabitch!" The intruder screamed into the night, stomping his feet and kicking at the sandstone barrier. "I'm gonna skin you alive and hang your hide out to dry, you murdering coward. You sick, cold sonofabitch!"

Ethan stood slowly and walked backward, then turned and climbed higher up the canyon. The drainage was getting steeper, the rocks growing larger and more difficult to climb or even go around. But he scrambled up another ledge and moved right until he could no longer see the restless search-light. The intruder had stopped screaming.

Ethan sat in the cool dark and tried to regulate his breathing. Calmness slowly replaced the panic he'd felt earlier. He should keep moving, but felt exhausted again. Who the hell is this guy?

He noticed a one-eighth moon above the far wall. Higher up, the drainage flattened out again. He walked carefully toward the sandy flats and began to cross them. A dark spot on the ground seemed to open up suddenly and he slid inside a freshly dug area about eighteen inches deep. He strained his eyes to see, but could not figure out what he'd stepped into.

Ethan listened closely but heard nothing. Oddly, the smell of spoiled pork reached his nose. The moon was hidden by rocks close at hand, which allowed him to see shadows a few feet away but nothing in the trench. He remembered his flashlight and pulled it out.

Unless the intruder found the same spot where Ethan had jumped, he would have to back track out of the fins, then find another way around and up the canyon. It was likely to take him a while. Ethan decided to use his flashlight for just a moment, to see where he was and which way to go. And what was causing that smell.

He swept the weak light over the ground and realized he was in one of the shallow, square-shaped holes he'd seen during the day, from part way up the plateau. He remembered realizing they were pits dug by artifact hunters. Looters.

He moved the light to his feet, then along one edge of the pit. As the light went farther up, his body went cold as snowmelt. His hands began to shake and he blinked, then blinked again. There, in the flickering dimness lay a body, bloated and blackened and swollen and stinking like raw sausage under a hot sun. The shirt had popped its buttons and lay open but looked familiar.

Lars.

CHAPTER 32

Anya's head pounded and her breathing became more shallow and irregular. Slowly, the world seemed to be re-entering her consciousness.

She opened her eyes and felt around with her hands. She was under a sleeping bag. Her fingers touched a bottle that sloshed with the sound of water. The view above her was blocked by a sandstone roof about four feet from her face. She was under some kind of ledge or in a cave.

The sound of boots scraping on the ground reached her ears, distorted by the rock walls into a series of loud, abrasive scratches. Someone was out there. Who was it? How had she gotten here? Should she call out?

Her throat was dry as the desert itself. Her legs tangled with the sleeping bag. She decided to move quietly from under the bag and to the edge of the opening. A ribbon of stars showed her the way. She sat up and looked around.

The sliver of a moon lit some of the ground farther away from her, toward the center of the side canyon and onto the water-flattened portion of the drainage. The rocks below her were dark as ink, only a few of their edges lined with light.

She heard footsteps again, farther up the canyon, moving away from her.

Her head throbbed and distracted her from thoughts of calling out. She drank mightily from the bottle, but her stomach rejected it moments later. She tried to calm her nerves. Whoever brought her here did it to keep her safe. She had a sleeping bag to keep her warm and water to keep her alive. She slowed her breathing and took small sips to avoid purging again.

Anya heard nothing further and began to get chilled. She rolled under the ledge and into the warm sleeping bag. This time, she slept deeply in the comfort of her own little space.

CHAPTER 33

Ethan's stomach clenched involuntarily and he vomited into the shallow pit. He wiped his mouth with the back of his hand, turned the light off and tucked it into a pocket. He stood there for a while, his hands on his knees, and tried to breathe.

The smell from Lars drove him out. He rolled out of the pit onto the ground and kept rolling until a batch of rabbit brush stopped him several yards away. He lay there taking shallow gulps of air, his ribs crushed tight by fear and revulsion and anger.

He practiced taking deeper, longer breaths and began to calm down. He had to think about what to do next. The intruder was still out there, no doubt coming up the canyon. This must be the man's dig site, which means he knows exactly how to get here. If he couldn't follow Ethan directly, he might come here and look for fresh tracks.

Just as he forced himself to stand, Ethan heard the unmistakable sound of boots shuffling behind him. He could see some open ground in the dim moonlight and moved in that direction.

He pulled the water bottle from at his waist and drank the last swallow as he walked. His body felt like every nerve had been crushed, every muscle lit on fire. He wasn't sure how much longer he could keep running. Now is the time, he thought, to hide and try an ambush.

He could hear soft, crunching sounds as the intruder stepped on dry brush, but the man's flashlight was turned off. Ethan tried to make out the meaning of shapes in front of him, whether they were rocks he should climb or avoid. He tried to remember the lay of the canyon he'd seen from on top of the plateau. If only he could reach that, he'd know where he was. But finding the warrior petroglyph that marked the only way up would be impossible. He knew the canyon had a crescent-shaped dry creek bed off to the side of the main drainage, just up from the square holes. He moved upward carefully and to his left, knowing sooner or later he should find it.

Light flashed behind him, from the intruder, in a search to Ethan's right. The man shuffled across the ground, following his lantern. Ethan used the sound to hide his own, dodging left and hurrying up an incline.

Ethan tread carefully over a long, flat rock then stepped down to a sandy basin. He turned and looked for the intruder's light, which was scanning below him, moving toward him again.

This seemed to be the sandy crescent. He moved quickly along the inside part of the semi-circle and then across to the main canyon wall. Large slabs of sandstone had fallen from above and were jammed against the wall along the bottom. He could see just enough to find a spot he could climb.

Shit, he thought, he'd forgotten to hide his tracks in the sand.

Quickly, he took off his shirt and trotted back across the area by memory. Just then, he heard the intruder stumble on some rocks and curse, his light flashing over Ethan's head.

Ethan bent down and walked backward, erasing blindly where he had just walked. The intruder kept cursing at something, then seemed to be moving quickly again. He'd reached the flat area.

Ethan hurried faster yet, dragging and swinging his shirt until he felt solid rock beneath his feet. The man's light swung fully to the right, then left as he advanced along the center of the crescent.

Ethan moved between two of the fallen rocks, climbing higher, searching for a way up above the man's line of sight. When he found one, he pulled himself several more feet up the edge and squirmed onto a flat spot that leaned into the canyon wall. The light probed the area but Ethan had found a dark spot about seven feet above the level ground. He curled into a ball and waited.

CHAPTER 34

Ethan must have blacked out. He'd had no real food for close to twenty hours and very little water. Adrenaline alone had kept him running until he found his small ledge and collapsed. He woke to light and thought for a moment the intruder had found him. But the light was gentle and diffuse. The sun had risen into the sky, but not yet reached beyond the distant eastern rim. He lay still and listened, wondering where the intruder was searching and whether Anya was getting better, or getting worse.

His muscles seemed locked into position. He pushed his legs straight and rolled onto his back. Everything ached. He remembered Lars, shoved into place in a shallow grave, bloated and cooked by the sun. He shivered and drove the image from his mind.

He wriggled his shoulders to a more comfortable

position and stared upwards.

Monolithic sandstone towered above him, its serrated upper edge defined by the deep, unreachable blue of space. Two of the local crows came into view, spiraling lazily below the rusty rim, quiet this time, too sleepy to gossip. After a bit, he sat up and unhooked his water bottle. Empty. He peered over the edge.

Below him was a bumpy patch of ground edged with prickly pear cactus. The area pointed like a finger to the sandy crescent he remembered crossing last night. He searched the dirt for footprints, but saw not even his own. He remembered he'd swept them with his shirt.

A singular cliff, part of the greater canyon wall, curved toward the east. Perhaps it was passable to the north. He remembered seeing a seep of water when he was on the plateau, not far from here. It was just above the sandy wash, on the right side going up the canyon.

He had to drink, and soon. He'd heard no sounds of human activity. The intruder could be long gone by now, or holed up somewhere waiting for him.

He willed his stiff muscles to move and sat up. From there, he scooted to the edge of the rock and lowered himself to the stepping stone he'd used last night. He turned and stretched his right leg to the ground, then spun and sat on the loose dirt at the bottom.

He began to breathe more regularly, stood, and walked at an even pace toward the edge of the level sand. He peered around the corner and searched quickly up and down the area. The old creek bed was dotted with cheat grass and small cactus, but otherwise empty. A large jumble of rocks accumulated at the center of the semi-circle, but the view dropped off beyond the flat to the south. He stood near the top of the dry bed and picked his way along, walking on rocks when he could, to avoid making footprints easy to follow.

Ethan walked a hundred yards or so, now well past the crescent itself. The canyon walls seemed to merge into one great wall with nowhere to go and from here, it looked like a dead-end, a box canyon. But he knew the seep was nearby. When he was on the high plateau, it seemed like an easy reach. From here, he had to search for passage to higher ground and hope he picked the right path.

He worked his way from boulder to boulder. After a bit, he came to a minor clearing and moved up it, stepping around the larger rocks piled along the way. The canyon was still in shadow there, the sandstone cool and comfortable to the touch. A house-sized rock lay in front of him. There, on the side, two wavy lines were etched into the stone. A petroglyph, way the hell up here. When he walked around the simple rock art, a stunning green patch of life appeared fifty yards farther up. The seep.

He hurried closer to the spot. Bright green moss and tiny ferns, completely out of place in this massive desert, clung happily to the moistened rock. Water dripped from a curve in the stone, watering another colony of thirsty ferns below it.

Ethan caught the cold water in his hands and rubbed them hastily together, then onto his face. He moved under the dripping desert water, closed his eyes, and felt it smacking his open lips. Water was life itself.

CHAPTER 35

Bobby cursed his bad luck. He'd almost had that sonofabitch last night. But the asshole had escaped from a dead end trail by climbing over the edge. Bobby had hurried back out of the narrow fins and searched the ground for a way around, but found none. But he knew the man he was going to kill could not be far away. The canyon was impassable just a mile or so farther up. Bobby was on the downslope. As long as Bobby did not let him slip past, the asshole was trapped.

He stood and spun his arms over his head to warm up. He checked his .38. Three shots left. He put the gun and shoulder harness back on. He could sure go for a stack of pancakes right now with syrup, coffee, toast and eggs, but he knew he'd have nothing to eat this morning. There was no sense thinking about it, but he was. His water was half empty, but he was thirsty, so he drank it all. Bobby was going to end this soon, before the sun was high. Then he would go back to Boss and tell him what had happened to Harold and Trevor, and how he had made it right. He shouldn't just tell Boss, he should show him. Maybe he should bring him that asshole's head in a bag. That would really impress his uncle. With Harold and Trevor gone, it was time for Bobby to move up to right hand man. He just had to prove it to Boss.

And he was ready.

CHAPTER 36

Tim took the wool ski hat off his head and replaced it with the rafting company's baseball cap. He rolled out from the rock he'd slept next to and looked around.

Mourning doves cooed lower in the canyon. A tiny lizard did push-ups on a stone. Tim stood and stretched. He'd stopped hiking late last night. He needed some rest and more time to think. He convinced himself he'd over-reacted to the unusual sound the night before - it could have been rock cleaving from the cliff. And wandering around in the dark had its hazards: you could easily trip and sprain an ankle or pull a groin muscle. Out here, that could be life threatening. Of course, the rafting group waited for him far below, down by the river. He needed to return uninjured and take them all out of the canyons and back to town. He'd left Norma more or less in charge. She could keep the group together and make sure they got fed until he got back.

He'd decided how to get through Black Heart rapids, once they were all back on the water. It was by far the most challenging part of the run. He'd row through it with the first raft, tie it off below, hike back up, then take the second one through. He could do that at Mother-in-Law rapid too, if he needed to.

He ate a power-bar and drank half his water, knowing his body would need it for the hike up the canyon. He looked around to get his bearings, then strolled out into the open and moved steadily up the drainage.

Thirty minutes later, he found the truck-sized boulder where he'd left Anya and Ethan and walked around it to the upslope side.

"Hey, Anya…" He stopped in mid-sentence. They were gone.

Tim searched the rock again, making sure it was the right one. But the shape and size were unmistakable. Ethan had said he'd found the golden button right there, in a sandy spot at the base of the stone. He scanned the ground for footprints. It seemed like the earth had been disturbed, but he could see no clear shoe or boot marks. He kept his eyes downward and walked in a semi-circle around the large rock, wider and wider. But there was nothing he could follow.

He raised his eyes to the rocks and crevasses above and below the truck-sized rock but found no sign of them. Damn it, they could be anywhere. The more disturbing question was, why had they moved? Had they covered their tracks? Had someone else come up the canyon last night, after all?

Had Anya woken up? He resisted the urge to call her name. Until he knew what else, or maybe who else, he was dealing with, he'd best keep his mouth shut. Damn it to hell.

He looked around one last time. They most likely went higher up. If they'd come down the canyon, he would have heard them from where he'd slept, so he began a steady pace to the northeast.

A quarter mile up, Tim came to a flat area under the west wall of the canyon. As he rounded a large rock, he saw two shallow, square shaped pits and stopped cold. In one of the pits was a body. Instinctively, he knew it was a man and that he was dead. The shape was swollen out of proportion. A shirt on the body looked familiar.

Christ, it was Lars.

He was going to have to be quicker than he'd thought.

CHAPTER 37

"Tim will be back later this morning with Anya and Ethan and he can organize a search," Norma assured them.

They'd all woken without the usual call for "coffee!" from their guides. Instead, Norma had made hot water for tea and they'd settled for cream cheese and bagels for breakfast.

"It's not like Lars to miss a meal," Carter scratched his forehead. "I don't even remember seeing him last night. Do you?" He turned to Lisa.

"I thought I saw him at the rafts, but it could have been Darren. It was kinda dark by then." She tucked her hands in her pockets.

"I went to my tent after I finished cooking the chicken last night. It was dark. I had to use my flashlight. I figured he ate while I was getting warmer clothes on," Norma said. "We were all so tired, we hardly talked to each other."

Carter tilted his head toward the sky and ran his hands through his hair. "I can't just sit here."

"But Tim wouldn't want us to split up," Norma put her hands on her hips.

"We've been up for over an hour and Lars isn't in his tent," Carter replied. "We could at least look around…"

Darren and Millie listened from a short distance. Millie kneaded her fingers on an empty mug and looked at her husband.

"We'll look back this way," Darren said, pointing toward their tent. Without another word, they stood and began walking away from the others.

"Weirdos," Carter mumbled under his breath.

Lisa looked to Carter, then to Norma.

"You and Lisa stay here," Carter nodded. "If anyone comes back, whistle as loud as you can a few times. I'm going to walk back to the baño and then keep on going, upstream."

"You shouldn't be hiking around alone," Norma warned.

He rolled his eyes.

She folded her arms and grunted.

Carter strode to his sleeping bag, grabbed his water bottle, and worked his way toward the portable toilet hidden behind the tamarisk. A narrow trail continued past the baño and wound its way through the brush and into an open area secluded from view. The path led to the base of some low cliffs, where it disappeared, but the rocks were broken in places and a wide ledge led gently upward. There might be a good view from on top, he thought, scrambling up.

He huffed his way to the crown of the outcrop, about fifty feet above the water, caught his breath for a moment, and shuffled carefully to the brink to peer over. The broad river powered through the canyon, curving away upstream, roiling away downstream. Sheer cliffs rose from the opposite shore, unbroken all the way to the morning sky. He turned and scanned the ridges and cliffs on his side of the canyon.

"Lars!" He yelled several times, shifting the direction of his call each time.

No replies, no flashes of metal, no movement anywhere.

"Damn it, Lars."

Rough ground stretched below him to a shelf that extended a half mile upstream. He made his way down to the edge, which ended abruptly about eight feet above the river. He turned toward the broadest part of the flats, took two steps forward, and heard a swarm of summer locusts beating their wings. He looked to the ground. No, not locusts. Curled tightly under a block of sandstone, an indignant snake shook its rattle defiantly, cold black eyes glaring at him.

"Shit!"

He jumped back nearly a foot then began a slow retreat to the lip of the shelf. He watched the snake intently, expecting a strike at any moment.

Then his left foot slipped off the edge of the low cliff, slamming his hand into the dirt, spinning him off the rock and down toward the churning river.

He had time for one quick breath before he hit the water with a slap and plunged below the surface. Stunned, he stayed suspended for a moment in the river's icy embrace. Then he kicked his feet and reached his arms toward the air he desperately needed.

His head broke the surface and he gasped for breath. He saw the shoreline moving quickly past and swam with all his strength toward solid ground. He heard Norma's voice getting louder and the tops of the cottonwoods come into view. With a deep sense of relief, he felt his toes touch the ground beneath him. He struggled toward the rafts, walking and swimming at the same time, the current still pulling him along.

"Carter!" Norma yelled again.

Gradually, his waist, and then his thighs, rose above the water-line. He trudged the rest of the way to shore and put his hands on his knees to rest.

"Are you all right?"

"Yeah," he panted. "Just took an unexpected swim," he said between breaths.

"Well, go on over to one of the chairs. I'll find a towel so you can dry off," Norma pointed.

He stood up and waited until his heart stopped pounding. "Holy shit, Norma." He looked at her. "I came on a rattle snake and stepped off the edge of a cliff." He pointed past the outcrop a quarter mile upstream.

"You sure you're OK?" she asked.

"My wrist is killing me," he shook his left hand, "but, yeah, I'm OK." He took another breath and looked around. "I yelled and yelled and looked all around from up there, but…"

"What?"

He shook his head. "No sign of Lars."

CHAPTER 38

Boss crumpled an empty coke can and tossed it in the trash. He flattened the local ranch map on his desk and studied it, looking for canyons similar in size and shape to the one where Bobby had found the sandal. Their dig site was on National Park land. He needed to help sell the lie that the sandal had been found on private land, instead, where removal of the artifact could be legal. He'd known the owner of the ranch on the map for decades and more than once had talked him into signing an affidavit that the owner had found an artifact himself and sold it to Boss. It was all part of the paperwork Boss provided to buyers in the trade. Once the artifact and its provenance went to a private collector, often that was the end of it. But, sometimes, the collector re-sold it, or died and left it to heirs who wanted to sell. Boss could care less about the re-sales, but no one wanted the feds to come knocking. Proof of the location of the dig site was his get-out-of-jail-free card. And this particular owner was turning 87 years old this year and in poor health. No one could question the dead, not even the FBI, and by the time the artifact moved beyond the first collector, the affidavit would be irrefutable. He liked that word, irrefutable.

But Bobby, Harold, and Trevor should have returned yesterday to report on their progress and re-supply. It wasn't like Harold to disobey instructions. Even if they had a problem of some sort, Harold would have sent someone out of the canyons and back to town to talk with him. Not even a wildly successful dig would delay them this long. No, something was wrong.

A van door slammed out back. Boss folded the map and slid it into the top drawer. He sat behind his desk.

"Boss? You here?" The back door creaked open.

"Come on in, Paul."

He moved through the short hallway to the living room Boss used as his office.

Boss pointed to the chair opposite his desk. Paul nodded a hello and sat down. It was nearly seven in the evening and the air was starting to cool.

Paul's eyes were small and set close on either side of the beak of his nose. When he looked at you, one eye aimed a little high and to the right, like he was seeing someone behind you. Though he hadn't shaved in days, his light blonde hair made it hard to notice. He brushed red dirt off his shirt and slapped the dust from his hat.

Paul was not a member of his crew, exactly, but Harold had gotten to know him pretty well. Boss had used him for a few errands now and then, transporting some of his less expensive artifacts. Paul could be unpredictable at times, and Boss had seen him display a violent temper. But he could handle gnarly, class IV whitewater and stay alive in the backcountry. Paul was tough and agile. It was time to trust him with something bigger.

"Paul, I have a job for you." Boss folded his hands together and leaned forward.

"Sure..."

"Listen, this could be really serious. Three of my regular crew have gone missing. I need you to find them and report back to me. And I need you to move fast."

Paul nodded. Boss described the location of the dig site and reminded Paul where to get onto the river and where to get out.

"You'll need to kayak this trip, cause you need to book-it down river and stay out of sight, if you can."

"Sure, I know just where that canyon is, and the beach that's there on the down-river side." He scratched his ear.

"I need you to get there fast as you can and find them. You know Harold. Trevor and Bobby are there with him. This is a very important site, Paul. You need to see what the hell is holding them up and get back to me ASAP. Be prepared for trouble. Take your pistol."

"Always."

"And cell phone, so you can call me as soon as you're in range. That's usually on top of the first ridge on the road back to town. Stop on top and try calling me. If that doesn't work, keep going and try again."

Paul nodded.

"Paul," Boss stood and put his hands behind his back. "I want a full report as soon as you return. A full report." He straightened his back.

"Yes, sir." Paul stood. "I'll get ready tonight and be on the water by sun up. Should be at Horse Canyon by day after tomorrow."

"Good man." Boss motioned Paul to the back door. Paul pulled his hat on, set his jaw tightly, and marched out, the back door slamming shut behind him.

Boss wandered over to the air conditioner. He'd commanded a full report. He allowed himself a quick smile and adjusted the dial.

CHAPTER 39

Bobby stayed as far from the pits as he could. He did not care to see Lars's body again. Besides, those pits were an utter waste of time. Harold had insisted on being methodical, which was fine. But after two days of digging, sifting the sand and dirt, and filling it back in, he was completely frustrated. He'd been so sure the ancient sandal he'd found last year was from that flattened area of the canyon. But aside from a couple of broken pieces of chert, they'd found no evidence of Anasazi activity. Nothing they could bring back to his uncle. It pissed him off.

And now his companions lay dead in their sleeping bags. If he'd not been restless that night, he would be dead, too. All for nothing. Not a decent arrowhead, not another sandal. Nothing.

He reached an area where a side drainage entered the main one and worked his way up the center, noting a sandy crescent- shaped flat to his left. The two drainages joined each other a hundred yards or so higher. He stopped to survey the area and catch his breath. It looked vaguely familiar to him. Was this where he'd found the sandal last year?

From here, the canyon seemed to be boxed in by high walls. A jumble of giant rock to his left might be passable for a bit and could be hiding the sonofabitch he's going to shoot in the head. He smiled at the thought and turned in that direction.

****

Ethan swallowed another mouthful of cool water from the dripping seep. He moved to the side and opened his water bottle. It would take a few minutes to fill.

Except for the game trail on the plateau he'd explored earlier, this tiny alcove was hidden from almost any point of view. Above, the sky narrowed into a twisting river of blue. Ahead seemed impassable, but he'd been learning how deceptive looks could be in these canyons. His bottle was half-full now, the sound of water dripping into water a welcome, healthy noise.

Tiny snail shells lay at the bottom of a lip of rock. They and the small area of grass and ferns seemed so foreign, so out of place in this Mars-like terrain.

When the bottle was nearly full, he pulled it back and screwed the lid on tight. He turned and slid a couple of feet back to the bottom and looked toward the house-sized rock with the wavy-line petroglyph on the other side.

There stood Bobby, right next to the large stone, a smile on his face, his silver pistol aimed at Ethan's chest.

CHAPTER 40

"Holy…" Ethan shuffled and slipped to the ground. His breath came in short bursts, his eyes wide.

"Got you, you little shithead," Bobby said calmly. "Thought you could get away from me, did you?"

"What do you want?" Ethan's words rushed together.

"I want you to point your gun at me so I can shoot you cold dead."

"I – I don't have any gun. What are you talking about?"

"Sure you do, you little shitfaced coward. You shot my partners in the head with it. Trying to jump our claim, steal our find?"

"Honest to God, I don't know what you're talking about, and I don't have any gun." Ethan rose to his knees, holding his hands and arms out to demonstrate.

"You left it somewhere, just out of reach. Want to

go for it? Go ahead, I'll give you a couple seconds. Go get your gun and I'll shoot you dead."

"I told you, I don't have any gun."

"This is for shooting my friends, my partners. You shot them in their sleep, you sick bastard. At least you're going to die awake. You know that justice is being done." Bobby raised the gun, pulled the hammer back and aimed at Ethan's head. A movement to the side caught Ethan's eye.

Pow!

A shock wave struck the little alcove and Bobby's head jerked unnaturally to his right, his cheek pressed to his shoulder, his arms suddenly loosened, and he dropped like a wet rag.

Ethan stared, dumbfounded, at Bobby's contorted form, watching for movement. Then he twisted to his right and saw Tim standing there, a .22 pistol in hand.

"Holy shit, Tim. You just saved my life."

"Yeah, well..."

Ethan stood up slowly. "What the hell..." He stared at Bobby's motionless body. He could see where the .22 had entered the side of his head. Ethan looked to the ground, squeezed his eyes shut for a moment, and tried to clear his head. "Thank god you got here when you did."

Tim kept the gun at his side.

"I didn't know you guys, you river guides, carried guns on these trips."

"Well, I keep one handy, but out of sight. You never know when an emergency can come up." He waved the pistol at Bobby's body.

"Sure."

Suddenly, a realization hit him.

CHAPTER 41

Bobby thought Ethan had shot his partners in the head. In their sleep, he'd said. Tim had a pistol and a practiced aim. Had Tim done it? What about Relic?

Tim seemed to notice the emotion sweeping over Ethan's face and stepped closer to him. "What's wrong, Ethan?"

"What's wrong? You just shot a guy right in front of me."

"He was ready to kill you."

"I know, I know, it's all just such a shock. It's too much to take in all at once." Ethan looked at his feet.

"Well, I think I know what was going on, Ethan. This guy was out here looting Indian artifacts. There's a big black market for the right kind of stuff, maybe like that button you found."

Ethan looked back up at Tim, whose hand was outstretched. "Do you still have it? I'd like to take another look."

Ethan pulled it slowly from his pocket, glanced at it, and put it in Tim's open hand.

"That was easy," Tim said.

"What?"

Tim raised the pistol to Ethan's head.

"What the fuck?" Ethan shouted, stepping back, disgusted with himself for doubting his own suspicions. "Did you shoot those other guys? The ones he was talking about?" He pointed to Bobby's body.

"Sure. This is a competitive enterprise, Ethan."

"Are you nuts? Really this nuts?" Ethan's voice raised an octave.

"You were a big help to me, Ethan. I had no idea this canyon had anything valuable in it. When you wandered off the trail, Anya worried about you. You'd become our problem, an unexpected guest on the rafting trip. She had to go up to find you. When she didn't come back, I went looking, too, and found the both of you."

"Shit." It was all Ethan could think to say. He started shifting his weight from foot to foot.

"Then you found this so-called button. By the way, it's not a god-damned button, Ethan, it's a piece of headgear. Pounded out of gold by Aztec hands. Proof they ranged this far north during the height of their reign, taking crops and prisoners as they went. It's the find of the century. If there was a battle up here, there could be leather shields, sandals, tools, knives, mummified remains, and more."

Ethan stopped moving and stared at Tim. "And Anya?" He raged. "You don't dare hurt her!"

"Anya? No, of course not. She doesn't know about your little button, only that somebody hit her from behind."

"You're a sonofabitch," Ethan shouted. "You can't let the police come back up here, they'd find your precious site, you know that. They'll have to investigate."

Tim thought for a moment. "I'll just tell them this Ethan guy did it. This Ethan guy, officer," Tim lowered his pistol and lapsed into an imagined dialogue. "He just appeared out of nowhere with some crazy story about a mountain bike accident. I never really believed that story. He was all cut up in places, but that must have come from the digging. He was digging for artifacts with this guy," he pointed at Bobby, "and must have had a falling out. Seems they weren't finding anything at all. There's never been a find up in this remote canyon, just the stone ruins right there along the river. It's crazy to be looking in this desolate place. These guys killed Lars too, when he stumbled on their dig. That part, Ethan, is probably true," Tim grinned.

Ethan sucked in a long breath.

"I came along, officer, following the sounds of people running up this direction, when I saw Ethan shoot his partner in the head. I hid until Ethan walked away, over there to get water, then I came out and grabbed that guy's .38. Ethan charged at me. I had no choice but to shoot him."

Tim stepped back, reached down and took the silver pistol from Bobby's grasp. Tim tucked the .22 into the front of his pants.

"You must have shot those poor bastards in their sleep, Ethan, except that this one got away and chased you up here. I heard shots. I was worried about Anya. We still didn't know if she was dead or alive."

Ethan wanted to vomit.

"Don't worry, I'll put your fingerprints on the .22 after you're dead." Tim lowered his head to check the .38. "I don't ever carry a gun on these trips, officers," he said, lapsing into dialogue again. "Too dangerous around these tourists, and the teenagers they bring with them. No, officer, never seen that .22 before in my life. Never seen that .38 either, till I took it off of this guy," he waived toward Bobby, "to defend myself from that psycho," he pointed to Ethan.

Ethan's stomach clenched again and his breathing stopped.

CHAPTER 42

Tim turned at the sudden sound of boots across the rough ground behind him. He listened intently, staring at the trail.

Bile rose in Ethan's throat, his rheumy fear stiffening and searing to a burnt-red anger. He tensed his legs and rushed forward, tackling Tim with all he could muster, the two of them flying to the ground, the pistol spinning from Tim's hand as they hit, Ethan struggling to keep his weight on Tim's chest, Tim reaching, pounding relentlessly on Ethan's back, driving the air from his lungs.

Relic leapt from the top of the house-sized boulder and rolled in the dirt. He slid close to the combat, smashing his fist into Tim's cheek, driving his temple hard into the ground. Tim's body went slack, his arms suddenly limp on Ethan's back, his hat spinning upside down in the dust.

Ethan scrambled up, his chest heaving, and he slowly backed away from Tim.

Relic rested his hands on his knees. He smirked at Ethan and gave a quick wave.

Ethan stared at him like he was seeing a ghost.

Relic reached for the .38 and, for a moment, Ethan's blood stopped coursing. Relic tossed the pistol into the rocks and it clattered between them with an un-natural, metallic echo.

"Damned snub-nosed," he said. "Always been more of a long-barrel man myself." He stood and walked back toward the large rock where he'd left his daypack.

"Shit, there, Relic." Ethan shook his head. "You've got the timing of a..."

"What?" Relic put his pack back on and walked closer to Ethan. "I tried to get here sooner, but I had to hold back to stay outta sight." He pointed at Tim a few yards away. "Guess it's a good thing he heard me, though."

Ethan shook the feeling back into his arms and grinned with relief.

"How many times do I have to save your sorry ass?" Relic asked.

"I guess just as many as it takes..."

"Well, hell, then..."

Tim suddenly shook his head, eyes clamped shut.

Ethan and Relic stood paralyzed, watching him come rapidly to life.

Tim felt along the ground for the .38. When he didn't find it, he reached under his shirt for the .22, wrapping his fingers around the barrel. A moan of pain modulated into a rising roar of anger.

"Shoulda kept that pistol," Relic scolded himself. He grabbed Ethan by the arm and led him up the narrow canyon, their escape propelled by the energy of a screaming killer.

They ran quickly over the flattest part of the drainage and through a jumble of rock, stopping at a plug of blood-red sandstone that ended the canyon like an immense period.

"We're trapped!" Ethan said, adrenaline feeding his panic.

"No. Follow me," Relic said. He stepped over loose scree to the side of the hulking stone. Boot-sized rocks had been jammed between it and the high cliff wall. He reached up and began to climb them like stairs, leaning forward as he went, keeping his hands on either side of the rock walls for balance. In moments, he was above the huge stone and turning out of view.

Tim had stopped yelling.

Ethan followed Relic up the odd stairway, haste making him skin his knees and knuckles. At the top, a narrow ledge led to their left. He slid his feet along the rock, kicking pebbles and dust off the edge.

Relic turned to Ethan and waved him forward. Ethan nodded and moved quickly along the path as it rose along the cliff. He could hear Tim moving and climbing below them, grunting with effort.

Relic disappeared around the curve of cliff ahead of him. Ethan moved more slowly as the ledge narrowed to the width of his shoe. A few yards ahead, the cliff above him yawned toward and over the trail, making it impossible to stand up. Ethan squatted low and shuffled along the dusty path, sweat running down his face.

Shortly, the cliff leaned away from the trail again and Ethan stood up. The ledge rose higher over steps of rock two and three feet high. He toiled to another level and tried to catch his breath.

"Keep going," Relic nearly whispered. Ethan could not see him, but knew he was close by, around the bend. He moved about two yards ahead when the ledge suddenly thinned to a few inches. Ethan stopped to get his bearings.

To his right was the high cliff, smooth as a polished apple as far as he could see. It must rise all the way to the top of the mesa. To his left was the little canyon they'd come up, five hundred feet straight down, directly beneath him. He put his hands on the rock wall to steady himself. One slip here would end it all.

He examined the skinny ledge for toeholds. Farther along, he could see where it widened again to about two feet. A veritable freeway over there, he thought. One or two steps were all he needed to cross the compact bridge.

He stared ahead and slightly downward, just enough to see the tops of his feet. In one, two, quick steps, he reached the other side.

He heard Tim reach the narrow ledge behind him. Without turning, Ethan hurried forward and around another bend in the trail, just out of sight.

CHAPTER 43

A low ridge appeared unexpectedly in the narrow path and Ethan scrambled over it. He reached a remarkably open, level area that ran to what seemed like another dead-end, where the cliff began a vertical climb to the top of the canyon rim. Relic leaned against the cliff at the far side, his arms crossed.

"Now what?" Ethan asked.

"You go on ahead and I'll slow him down."

"Ahead where?" Ethan looked about the scattered sand and towering walls.

"Here." Relic turned and pointed to a row of footholds carved into the bare sandstone. "This route curves up, to the left, where there's another ledge."

Sure enough, a dozen or more shallow grooves had been ground into the solid surface, rungs on a stone ladder. The ancient ones had chiseled into the cliff with harder stones like granite, and then hollowed them into serviceable hand and foot holds. Incredible. What made them go to such extremes? What danger did they need to escape so high above the canyon floor? Or was it just a practical way to the top, a way to reach other canyons in these massive lands?

Ethan heard Tim cursing at the narrow ledge, deciding whether to cross it.

Relic pointed up. "There's a granary there too, you'll see it on the right after you get onto the ledge."

"I'm not leaving you here alone…"

"No." Relic moved away from the cliff. "No time…"

Tim had stopped his cursing.

"But…"

Relic gathered a handful of rocks at his feet and positioned himself just beyond the curve of the cliff, where Tim would be coming. "Better get!"

They heard Tim scrape along the sandstone as he shuffled along the narrow footing in the trail.

Ethan swallowed hard and gazed up at the shallow holds in front of him. He started up, moving as quickly as he dared.

CHAPTER 44

Tim balanced on the shallow ledge as Relic pelted him with rocks. "Shit!" Tim yelled, shielding his face.

The sound of Tim's voice made Ethan's heart skip, his left hand slipping from its hold. He forced himself closer to the rock and reached for the next carve-out. When he had it, he risked a quick glance behind him.

Tim scrambled backward on the narrow shelf, twirling his arms to keep his balance. Once he was beyond the corner, he cursed again and slowly reached his pistol around the cliff for a shot.

Relic had already moved and Tim must have sensed it. He held his fire. Relic had changed his angle and hid behind a crack farther from Tim's view.

Ethan scrambled up the last hand hold and onto level ground, panting. He rolled himself over, farther onto the high ledge, and looked around. Next to him was a small granary, a semi-circle of neatly stacked and carefully mortared stone backed up against the cliff. Atop it sat a single flat stone shaped to fit on the lip of the storage. A lid. Sealed tight with mud that had dried over centuries, its contents still inside, its owners yet to reclaim it.

The soft scrabbling sound of someone climbing stone filled the air. Though Ethan could not see him, he thought it must be Relic. Ethan risked a look back from where he'd come.

Down below, Tim crab-walked closer to the exposed point on the ledge, then stood and went quickly to the large flat area, away from the edge. He kept one hand raised, to protect his face from flying rocks, but none came. He stopped and pulled the gun, looking around anxiously. Relic was gone.

To his left, Ethan could see Tim searching the ground, moving in and out of Ethan's sight. Not a good line of sight for throwing rocks, he thought.

Ethan heard the rushed sound of movement and a sudden stop. He moved several feet to his right and leaned over the edge at that spot as far as he could. Now he could see the downward curve of the steps and more of the clearing below. He pulled his head back and listened. Where, exactly, was Relic?

Tim found the ancient hand-holds and grunted in

surprise. He walked cautiously toward the sculpted ladder, scanning the area. Silence stilled the canyon. Then
Tim began to climb, keeping the gun in his right hand,
ready to fire.

Ethan could hear Tim's boots scraping rock as he
moved carefully higher. Ethan searched desperately for
a place to go. The flat spot where he lay also extended
away from the granary and farther up the canyon. Maybe it kept going or led to another path. Without Relic,
though, he had no way of knowing.

CHAPTER 45

Suddenly, Relic appeared at the far end of the area that was level with Ethan, doubled over, breathing hard.

"How did you…" Ethan lifted himself up and swung his feet underneath him, scattering pebbles and dust over the edge of the cliff.

Tim looked up just as sand bounced off the rock above. His eyes seared shut with the sting of fine dust. The pistol left his grip and wobbled on his fingers for a moment, dancing away from him, but his index finger looped through the trigger guard and the gun fell back into his hand. He tried to blink the sand from his eyes, reached too far for the handhold, and missed, his boot angled away from the step, slipping from under him.

The short scream hit Ethan like a punch.

Tim's body slapped the ground like wet cement on stone. Ethan's skin prickled, an awful silence drafting its way behind the broken sound.

Quietly, Ethan and Relic waited. The deep hush of a mausoleum filled the canyon.

Finally, they peered over the ledge. Tim's body lay down on the ground, his head twisted in a wholly unnatural bent.

CHAPTER 46

"Oh my god." Ethan slid to the ground.

Relic sat next to him and leaned against the cool sandstone. "We should stay here for a while."

Ethan nodded. He needed to process this new death, but was wracked with questions. He took a long drink and felt the weight of it in his stomach. They sat there for a long while.

"Do you know what the hell is going on around here?" Ethan grimaced.

"Sure. You ought to know by now too, eh? What do you figure?"

Ethan took a deep breath. "A group of men have been digging for artifacts. I found one myself: a button-shaped piece of metal with etching on it. The rafting group ran into the men by accident…"

"Yeah, I'm sure they killed the guy with the

yellow hat."

"Lars," Ethan whispered.

"Didn't see it, but it must have been them. Nearly killed that young woman, too."

"Anya. You know about her?"

"I saw you find her. Later, I saw the tall guy," he motioned towards the body.

"Tim."

"Yeah, Tim, he went to you, then headed back to camp. He came back again to give you food and water, then returned to camp. I decided to follow him, since I knew you were OK." Relic wrinkled his nose.

Ethan looked at him. "What?"

"He acted real odd after that. Stopped a few times on the way back to camp, looking on the ground, checking around some of the rocks. He spent a short time in camp with the group, but after the sun went down, someone with a flashlight was moving around. It looked like Tim. He turned off his light for a while and went upriver, away from the rafters, along the flats - not into the canyons.

"I knew there were three men camped under a hidden overhang, right where the main canyon hits the river. About a half mile from the group of rafters. I followed at a safe distance till I heard two shots – two quick, little pops. I hightailed it back to the rafters and watched Tim walk right past them and keep on going. This time, he went up this side canyon." He pointed below them. "That's when I knew he was another looter, claim jumping the other three."

"You've been out there, in the canyon? The whole time?"

"This is one of my favorite canyons, and I had visitors." He grinned and pointed at Ethan. "Remember our talk a few days ago, up by my still?"

"Sure."

"You promised never to reveal me to anyone. Remember?"

"Yes, yes, of course." Ethan's lips tightened. "And I never will."

"Good man. I'd hate to have to poison you with wicked, canyon gin."

Ethan nodded, then stopped. "Actually..."

"Sorry, it's all stashed at the moment. But there's another promise I need from you..."

"Name it."

"You have the artifact on you?"

Surprised, Ethan shook his head. "Tim took it. It should be in his pocket."

"I need to rebury it."

CHAPTER 47

They went slowly down the ancient hand-carved stairs, facing the rock wall, finding each grove by the feel of their toes. When they reached the bottom, they were exhausted. Neither wanted to look too long at Tim, his hips twisted, his face in the sand.

"I need to find the artifact," Relic pointed at Tim. "Can you pull him away from the cliff, to straighten him out? That way, I can reach into his pockets."

Ethan wasn't sure he could do it. But if he waited too long, if he thought about it too much, the idea would be out of the question. He moved closer to Tim's body and reached for the flaccid arm.

It was the second time Ethan had seen a man die and the first time he'd touched the dead. He lifted the arm and pulled Tim over rough ground. The body snagged, then jostled past a rock, seeming to stir of its own volition. He leapt back-ward, spooked for a moment that Tim had come back from the dead to grab him.

"Let me help you," Relic took Tim's other arm.

In another moment, Tim was straightened on the ground and they laid his hands back into the dirt. Relic quickly felt through Tim's pockets and found the round metallic headpiece.

Relic stood for a moment, hands crossed in front of him, looking at Tim. He mumbled a quiet prayer in a language Ethan did not recognize, but he had no need to know the words. The meaning was clear and true. They stood for a minute in silence, their eyes on the ground.

"Tim said the artifact is Aztec head-gear," Ethan said, "or something like that. He said its proof the Aztec raided this far north, into Anasazi territory." Ethan looked up at Relic. "He called it the find of a lifetime."

Relic scowled and looked back at the body. His eyes narrowed into pencil-thin slits. "Well, Mr. Tim, this may complicate a few things for me."

"What?" Ethan asked.

"Let's sit over there."

Ethan was relieved to turn away. They walked to the ledge and went around a slight bend, just out of sight of the body. Relic pulled his water bottle out and they shared a swallow of the little that was left. They sat on the edge and looked out across the hot, still canyon.

"You can't tell anyone what you found here, or where you found it. I'm going to tell you something very important, so you understand that you must keep this promise," Relic spoke solemnly. "This will be your second promise, Ethan."

Ethan leaned forward.

"I saved your life. You owe me this."

"Yes, of course," Ethan nodded.

"Tim is about right. Some of my ancestors roamed all through these canyons and fought off the Mexica, later known as the Aztec, and many other invaders over the centuries. There were only a few of us, but we hid and fought and survive to this day. The so-called Anasazi you hear about are really Hisatsinom, ancestral Hopi."

Relic folded his hands.

"These looters, these dirty grave robbers, are part of the reason I'm here. To keep the secrets hidden from those who would steal history. But it's a living history - one that hasn't ended. One I'm only a little piece of."

Ethan folded his hands together.

"Time is paper-thin here, Ethan. You can reach right through it. You touch a granary, you reach the hands that made it twelve hundred years ago. That one behind us, above the stone steps, still has fingerprints in the clay. It hasn't been opened in ten centuries."

Ethan thought about that.

Relic stroked the thin, black hairs on his chin. "You'll need to go back to help Anya and the rafters, so they can move along. When you get back to town, you and she will have to tell the sheriff what happened to her, and to Lars, and Tim. They should come and investigate and take those dead men out of here."

"Yes."

"Ethan, the looters were digging in the wrong place. Where you found the head-piece is also out of place. It must have washed down there, maybe this spring. But you don't have to tell them about the head piece at all. Tim found the dig site, thought he'd take it from the others, and that's what happened."

"Do you think more will come back?"

"Not much doubt." Relic scratched at his beard. "Sometimes it's a bigger challenge than others."

"Guarding these sites?"

Relic nodded.

Ethan reached for the water and took another sip.

"What about Tim?" he pointed behind him.

"Tell them just the way it happened but leave a couple things out of the story. You got away from Tim down below and ran up here. You found the footholds then shimmied across the ledge and up the rock ladder. Tim was chasing you and he fell by accident. Just leave me and the head-piece out of it. It's the only way to protect this canyon. And... me."

"Speaking of which, what's wrong with you coming forward about all this? Don't tell me it's because you're running a home-made still on federal land..."

"I'm not sure the park service or the sheriff would really appreciate me. Besides, once I'm known to law enforcement, the news will get out there and people everywhere will be on the lookout. I can't do the work I do under a spot light. I need to be the unseen hermit, and I like it that way."

"And the still keeps you in gin and spending money?" Ethan grinned.

"Something like that. It's decent cover if I ever get caught protecting these sites too. I'm just a crazy old coot, drinking gin and howling at the moon."

"Are you sure it's just a cover story?" Ethan raised his brow. Relic smiled and slapped him on the back.

CHAPTER 48

"We have to go now," Ethan shifted, "and get back to Anya."

"*You* do," Relic said.

"Oh, well, yes."

"You have some scrambling to do first, to get down from here," Relic pointed.

"I do." Ethan looked at the cliff ledge they'd come up. The sooner I get it over with… he thought.

"Take your time. They don't call it slick-rock for nothing," Relic said.

"When will you get to rebury the… artifact?"

"Maybe I'll wait up on top for a few days, wait 'till the sheriff and others come and do their thing, then I'll come back down. I'll put it where it was before the big spring run-off moved it down the canyon, so it will be in a spot no one has thought to dig yet."

Relic and Ethan stood and shook hands.

"When you get back to the rafter's camp, would you leave my water bottle in the cliff dwelling there?" Relic asked. "Just tuck it away inside the door, not too obvious. I'll get it next time I'm there."

"Sure."

"I know you want to check on Anya, take her and the rafters out of here. By the time the sheriff gets here, I'll be long gone." He nodded up the canyon.

"Up there?" Ethan looked at the wall of rock and saw no way out. Blood-red sandstone curved high above them, a flattened hand outstretched to the sky.

"My ancestors found a way, and etched it with rock art. I've been up this way once before."

Ethan squinted. "You said that earlier - something about some of your ancestors…"

"One of my grandfathers was Hopi," he said. "My other was Scottish and Welsh - a looney combination," he grinned. "Where do you think I got my recipe for gin?"

Ethan could not find the words. In the end, he just said, "Thank you."

Relic winked at him and headed back toward the hand-carved stairs. Ethan shuffled across the high ledge as it rounded the cliff. He kept his momentum crossing the narrow part of the path and slid his bottom down the series of stones to the lower level. Soon, he was above the giant plug that seemed to end the canyon on their way up. He stepped carefully down the stones jammed into the crevasse by the ancestral Hopi and found himself back on the canyon floor.

His knees grew rubbery as he stepped over and around the rocks and thought about what had happened. He followed the drainage down, avoiding Bobby's body and the sandy crescent- shaped area. Farther along, he saw the dig site and worked his way to the far left to avoid seeing Lars again.

Past the dig site, he cut across a flat area, moving right, searching for the overhang where he'd left Anya. He did not have to look for long. There she sat, legs swinging from the ledge like a little girl's. She waved.

Relief washed through him, and he waved back, smiling.

Ethan hurried up the slope, scrambled past the limestone lip, and went on hands and knees to the sand-stone ledge. He turned and sat next to Anya, panting.

She smiled at him like the sun.

He caught his breath, nodding at her. "So, how are you feeling?"

"Better now, thanks to you, I guess." She rubbed the back of her head. "When I woke up, I wasn't sure what was going on, so I just kept my eyes shut for a while. I guess it was after you'd left, I heard someone walking in the dark, but I wasn't sure who it was, so I kept quiet. Later on, I sat up, threw up, then tried to get my nerves under control."

"Sounds right."

"You left me with food and water, bless you."

"Sure. I was worried you might never wake up." His voice faltered; he regretted being so obvious.

"You pulled me up here? Off the trail and under this ledge?"

"Yes."

"I wondered. Well, you saved my life, Ethan. I don't know what to say…"

He stirred up the courage to say what he meant. "It's a life worth saving."

She reached across and hugged him tightly. In a wave of relief more deep than he expected, he returned her embrace.

Ethan leaned back and steeled himself. He told her about the looters, and, sadly, Lars. He explained how he'd been chased through the night, leading one or more of them away from Anya's hidden ledge. He told her Tim had killed the other looters so he could have the whole site to himself, then how Tim had attacked Ethan with the same pistol he'd killed the others with, but Ethan had gotten away. Then he told her about the narrow ledge along the cliff and the footholds carved into the smooth sandstone and how shallow and slick they were.

"Tim slipped on the steps when he was close to the top. Anya, he fell and was killed there."

She took a deep breath and touched her hand to her chest.

"Did Tim kill Lars too?"

"Tim told me he'd killed the others, but not Lars."

"He talked to you about it?"

"Right before he was going to shoot me." He thought briefly of Relic and hurried through his lie of omission. "He turned around and I tackled him. He was knocked out for a minute. That's how I got away, when I went farther up the canyon."

"Oh, god."

"We need to get to the boats and get everyone out of here."

Anya's lips tightened with resolve. "You're right. But it will be dark before we'll have time to break camp. There are rapids ahead too. We can't run them in the dark. We'll have to sleep here, I mean, where the camp is at now. We have an emergency satellite phone to call for help, but we shouldn't stay here any longer than we have to. We can ask for helicopter take-out a few miles down-river." Anya went quiet again for a moment. "I'll have to find a way to tell the others..."

Ethan looked across the narrow canyon. Though they were only a mile or so down the trail, the little group of rafters seemed a world away.

She looked into the distant sky, thinking. "Have you ever steered a raft through rapids?"

Ethan looked up at her and swallowed and he thought about something Relic had said. "I haven't had that particular human experience, yet."

She cocked her head at his choice of words.

"Let's get going." He put his palm in hers and pulled them along.

CHAPTER 49

Ethan followed Anya as she wound her way through scattered brush and stone. They spoke not a word.

Time wandered slowly back to the present as the ground leveled out and the smell of river water reached Ethan's nose. Cottonwood shadows had begun their long stretch across the grass. His thoughts shifted to the rafting group waiting at camp and the whitewater rapids they would face in the morning.

Carter appeared as they turned the corner. He waved, then trotted to the beach to gather the others.

Ethan decided to hold back a few yards as Anya quickened her pace. She shooed away chattered questions and went directly to one of the rafts. She hopped nimbly onto the outer tube, turned to the group, and balanced herself.

"I've got bad news," Anya began. Ethan listened as

she told them what had happened. Sadly, she said, Lars had been killed by the looters and Tim had fallen to his death on a cliff high up the narrow canyon.

Everyone seemed to stop breathing.

Almost in a whisper, she said Tim might have been a rival, a looter who wanted the site for himself, but that was not entirely clear.

Canyon air rushed across the water and shivered the cottonwood leaves.

Ethan could hardly listen any longer. He wandered to a rock above the beach and sat down. He could tell Anya was having a tough time, Millie and Carter and Norma throwing their questions at her.

After a bit, Anya finished talking and slid off the raft. She rifled through a blue dry bag lashed to the rear of the boat and seemed to find what she was looking for. She straightened up and spun a black, rectangular object over and over in her hands, searching it closely. After a moment, she put her fists on her hips and seemed to be cursing in frustration. She held up the satellite phone so Ethan could see it and mouthed the words: "He took the battery." Ethan shook his head. Tim had planned ahead.

An auburn sun laid its weary head on the high rim, squashing a final flare of light over the edge, leaving Ethan and the tiny group suddenly in shadow.

CHAPTER 50

After only three hours of sleep, Ethan woke abruptly. Whatever he might have been dreaming was already lost.

There had been no campfire, no jokes, no banter at the fringe of firelight, no flask of whisky passed between them. Stars shone like a distant highway at the edge of outer space. The Milky Way. There was just enough light to be able to see his way around the camp.

He wiggled out of his bag and moved it higher up the beach. It felt like every muscle in his body had been beaten with a rock. Someone was in a portable chair several yards up river; he could see movement and what looked like a lit cigarette. He stretched and then shuffled in that direction, longing for some human conversation.

He grabbed a camp chair along the way and then recognized the smoker as Carter. He sat next to him and said hello. Carter nodded and offered his joint to Ethan.

"Not in the mood," Ethan said.

"Takes the edge off, bro."

"Thanks anyway." He lowered himself into the canvas seat. "How are you doing?"

"My wrist still hurts."

"Your wrist?"

"Well, I went looking for Lars earlier, came on a rattle snake…"

"Oh?"

"Stepped back, slipped and fell on my hand, then into the river."

"Whoa…"

"Swam a little and made it back to shore."

"You're OK?"

"Yeah, I'll be OK. Better than Lars."

"No shit," Ethan whispered.

Carter took a deep pull on the joint and held his breath.

Ethan tried to clear his mind. He leaned forward, stretching his back. He wasn't sure if it hurt less to sit still or to keep moving.

Carter exhaled slowly. The joint smelled pungent, almost damp.

"What do think is really going on here, Ethan?" Carter coughed.

"There's a big black market in antiquities. Pueblo antiquities."

"I mean right here, right now." Carter turned in his chair and looked around. They were quite a distance from any of the tents or rafts. "I gotta tell you something. When I was walking up the canyon, the smaller one, not the one with the old moonshiner's place..."

"Yeah?"

"I saw a flash of light, like from glass or a mirror, up on the right side. I saw somebody move up there too, somebody maybe watching us."

"Who?"

"I don't know, man." He shook his head. "His hair was black, but I only saw him for a second or two. Ethan, he wasn't anybody from our group."

"When did you see this?"

"The day before yesterday. Seemed odd enough then, and now it seems like someone's been sneaking around, keeping tabs on all of us all this time."

Ethan thought of Relic. And the looters.

"Besides, if Tim was in on it, in on all this black market shit, who else is involved? That's what I'm thinking, bro. Who else is in on it?"

"Sure. Well, who else? What do you think?"

"Millie and Darren."

"Why?" He sat up.

"Have you seen how they act? They stay off to themselves all the time, they look like they're watching everything we do. I went for a walk this morning and they popped up, looking all guilty and shit. It's like they're following me around and messed up, got caught."

Ethan stayed quiet.

"When we heard that Tim was one of these looters, I could hardly believe it. He chased after you, bro. Tried to kill you, man, that's sick."

"Yes, it is." Ethan clasped his hands together.

"I trust you, bro." He put his hand on Ethan's shoulder and shook it gently. "But not Millie and Darren. You ever even see them kiss? Hold hands? I'm thinking they're not even married. They're here for something else. I just haven't figured it out, yet."

Maybe it was the marijuana making Carter paranoid. Ethan thought of the old joke – it's only paranoia if no one's out to get you. He shook his head at the cliché. Tim had blown a hole in the side of Bobby's head, all for whatever treasure he thought was up that side canyon. He pictured Bobby's body, suddenly drained of its electricity, its plug yanked violently from the source. His face had turned downward into the dirt. Blood had flowed across the sand in the shape of a funnel, widening with the distance.

And Tim. He had fallen to his death for the same treasure. He could see Tim's weirdly twisted torso, his bones turned to rubber. He recalled how it felt to pull Tim across the sand, to straighten out his body. He shivered.

Ethan didn't want to think about it anymore. He felt achy and sore. Now that he was up and about, he wished he'd stayed in the sleeping bag.

"I'm tired, Carter. Thanks for talking with me, but I think I'm going to go lie down again. I need some sleep."

"Watch your back."

"I will."

Ethan folded the chair and carried it with him. The river burbled and hummed through the cliffs and helped to calm his nerves. Tomorrow they would leave this camp, and the troubles of the dead, behind.

CHAPTER 51

Sunlight filtered through the cottonwood leaves and flashed across his face. After his visit with Carter last night, Ethan had not slept well. He sat up in his sleeping bag and drank a third of the water from his bottle.

Across the river, cliffs rose a thousand feet into the blue air. Morning sun glazed the high sandstone.

Ethan refilled the bottle from the cooler at the rafts and set off toward the cliffs down river from camp. Behind the cottonwoods, a well-worn trail led to the Pueblo ruins a few hundred yards away. In a few moments, he reached the largest structure overlooking the river and stopped.

He moved up to the opening and peered inside. What little he could see appeared to be empty of all but sand blown in on the winds. Light wriggled its way through a few small cracks in the mortar. Stones above the door were held in place by a longer stone that bridged the gap. Beneath that, a pair of wooden shafts the width of his thumbs supported the long stone. Aged to the color of bones, the wood was barely noticeable.

Ethan placed Relic's bottle, full of fresh water, behind the door on the left. He tucked it as far back as he could reach without touching or entering the ancient stone building.

He wondered if Relic would ever really retrieve it. But it was an especially valuable bottle, one with a filter down the middle of its throat, one that could save a person's life out here. A bottle that had kept Ethan alive. A bottle that had probably kept Relic alive.

Such a simple, priceless, thing.

He stepped back and stared at the well-built structure for a while longer, then turned and made his way back to camp.

The group was still quiet but in better spirits, nodding and greeting one another politely. Ethan ate breakfast until his stomach felt like a rubber balloon filled to bursting. Strong coffee filled in the few vacant places left.

Anya massaged the back of her head where the shovel had struck her and then looked at the group. She tapped a spoon against the frying pan to get everyone's attention. "I have a request this morning," she began.

Everyone moved closer.

"I need to know if someone would take one of the rafts through the rapids today."

Darren glanced at Millie.

"I would," Carter began, "but my wrist is still swollen from yesterday." He held up his left hand. "Hurts like the devil to move it."

"I'll do it," Ethan volunteered.

"No one *has* to do it, keep in mind. Only if you're sure you want to try it."

"Absolutely," Ethan said.

Anya smiled. "I'll take all the guests, so you won't have to worry about them," she said to Ethan. "And we'll load almost all the gear onto your boat." She nodded at the raft nearest him.

"Got it," he said.

In about thirty minutes, the camp was almost fully packed. Anya told Millie and Darren to keep the folding chairs on the beach while she took Ethan out into the water.

"For what?" Ethan asked.

"A rowing lesson. Hop onto the equipment raft with me and we'll get you the hang of this." She pulled her sunburnt hair into a ponytail and jumped into the raft. Ethan followed her and sat on the edge while she unhooked the oars and dipped them into the river.

"Sorry, you need to hop back out and push us off, then hop in when we're about a foot deep."

Ethan did as he was told and pulled himself back into the raft.

"Now," she said, "watch me."

Anya leaned forward, her arms down toward the boat, which left the wooden oars high out of the water. She then lifted her arms up, dipping the oars down and leaned and pulled them back and away from her. With each set of strokes, the raft pulled slowly upriver into a backwater that circled them gently around but kept them out of the main current.

"This is your power stroke. It takes you backward, so you have to look behind you. Put your whole body into it, not just your arms or you'll wear yourself out." When they reached the edge of the eddy, she worked the oars to turn them around.

"Watch again." She repeated the power strokes, moving to the shore, then turned around again. "Ready to try it?"

Ethan nodded and moved up to her spot. She handed the oars to him and moved out of the way. He lifted them into and out of the water, getting the feel of them, then dipped them into the river and pulled them back.

"Get your legs and back into it. More with your legs and back," she said.

He tried again and the raft moved noticeably backward as they spun toward the main current.

"OK, now row with just one oar, the left one, backward like you were doing with both of them. See how the raft moves?"

Ethan did as she instructed and felt the raft spin against the stroke.

"Now, when you are lined up where you want to go, remember your heading is behind you, then put both in the water and row. Adjust your direction with either oar and your power comes from when you row together, with both of them."

Ethan tried to maneuver, spun past where he wanted, countered with the other oar, then lined himself up with the shore and pulled hard three times. The raft took aim and moved slowly toward the beach and grounded.

"Not bad," Anya said with a smile.

He absorbed the warming praise, though he was sure he didn't deserve it.

Carter strode up to the raft and waded into the river. Anya nodded at him and he pushed them back into the water. The raft spun gently and when it lined up with the direction back to the main group seated on shore, Ethan put his back into it. To his surprise, the raft responded well and stayed on course to the other raft, where it bumped to a cushioned stop.

Anya patted Ethan on the back. "You're a quick study. You'll have it in no time." She jumped off his raft and motioned for the group to collapse their chairs, load them on, and get settled into her boat.

Ethan sat there, feeling the weight of the oars, glancing out into the main current.

Anya seemed to read his mind. "The water is a gentle flow here for about two miles, Ethan. Once we get out there, I'll take the lead, but let's stay close together for now. When we get close to the first set of rapids, I'll go farther ahead and scout them. If the water's high enough, they'll be no big deal."

"OK." Ethan realized his biggest mission was likely to be getting the raft to the right spot on shore. If he missed, the river would sweep him past the landing and into unknown currents all by himself.

"You'll go out first then just row upriver gently," Anya added. "I'll row downriver and go past you, to take the lead."

He nodded and watched the gurgling river.

"If I point somewhere, go in that direction. I will

always point you away from potential trouble. So keep an eye on me." She watched the group get settled into her raft. "All life jackets on and as tight as you can stand them?" She smiled.

Murmurs of agreement and tugs on the life preserver straps followed. Ethan double checked his own.

"Now see if you can row out without a shove-off from shore."

"All right." Ethan dipped his paddles into the shallow water and pulled awkwardly away from Anya. In a few moments, he was past the backwater and suddenly into the current. His heart began to race as he spun one hundred and eighty degrees and swept past Anya's raft and into the middle of the powerful river.

CHAPTER 52

Ethan seemed to be flying past the shore line, past the camp, past the tall cottonwood trees, level with the Pueblo ruin, then past it in only a few breaths. His was the only raft on the river and he felt a pang of loneliness.

The river turned tightly to the northeast. Around the bend, a whole new vista opened. Two buttes stood in the distance like the remains of giant castles, chess rooks with rough-hewn sides and high, flat tops. The canyon opened wide, a yawn in the huge plateau above them.

He lifted the oars, then dipped them in and pulled hard backward. Though the shoreline moved quickly, the water around his raft seemed almost motionless. He was in the flow now, and the water where he was rowing was calm and unhurried. He paddled his right oar until the raft faced downstream, then he rowed hard backward, upstream, as Anya had instructed.

"Nice work!" Anya cried from thirty feet away. Her voice startled him; he'd forgotten to look backward, the way he was going. She rowed past him in short order and spun her raft to move closer to his.

The group seemed happy to be on the water again. They were smiling and joking among themselves. Even Carter, so paranoid about them the other night, was laughing with Millie and Darren.

He looked behind and saw nothing of where they had camped, nothing of where he had met Relic or Lars or Tim.

"Try lining up toward either shore and rowing that direction. Then, turn a one-eighty and row to the other shore," Anya said.

Ethan nodded. He moved the oars in a clumsy mixture of moves that took the raft nowhere in particular. Frustrated, he lifted his left oar onto the raft, out of the water, and concentrated on rowing the right one until he spun the boat. When his back was aimed at the shore, he put both oars in the water and rowed across the water.

He looked over his shoulder and decided he was close enough. He then made the same maneuver with his left oar, spinning the raft to the opposite direction.

Anya rowed gently upstream, staying a dozen yards

away. Ethan rowed again. When he began to stray from his target, he stopped and used one oar to straighten, then resumed with both. He slid across to the other side and repeated the exercise. When he was half way across again, he centered the raft and caught his breath. He had begun to sweat, but it evaporated quickly in the desert breeze.

Anya gave him a thumbs-up signal. He smiled like it was his first time ever.

"Water," Anya reminded him and the group in her boat. "A gallon a day keeps the mortician away."

Ethan rested the oars on the sides of the raft and drank as much as he could. The river took them aimlessly down the wide canyon, spinning them slowly, displaying all there was to see, coming and going. Geese waddled in the mud along shore. Swallows spun in acrobatic flight inches above the water.

They floated on that way for nearly an hour when Anya roused herself into action and rowed closer to Ethan's raft.

"The first set of rapids is Black Heart rapids, around this bend," she pointed. "They're not difficult if you follow me through. We'll start left, then row river-right. That's it, simple. That one move and we're through. I think you'll have plenty of time, but don't dawdle, either."

"OK. Stay left for now?"

"Yes. You'll see a big rock on the right. As soon as you are even with it, start rowing toward it. By the time you get there, the river will have taken you past it. There's a series of rapids and a pretty big hole on the left, so when you get to the right, stay right and we'll be through in no time."

He took a deep breath. The sound of rapids was roaring around the bend and he suddenly wondered what kind of idiot he was.

CHAPTER 53

Paul stopped paddling and let the sleek kayak slow to match the river's pace. He set the paddle across his lap and flexed his long fingers and arms. The canyon was around the next bend, so he took a moment to catch his breath and drink more water. He'd worked hard to get here as quickly as he could. His muscles would be sore tonight, but they felt good.

He hugged the right shore, on the lookout for others. There, barely visible in the brush, were two light blue rafts; the ones used by Boss' crew. He pulled in next to them and wiggled out of his boat. No one seemed to be around. He stretched, removed his helmet and tied off his kayak. He refilled his water bottle from a three gallon bladder behind the seat in his boat and put a red daypack on his back. Then he reached into the recesses of the kayak and pulled out a purple rubber bag. He opened the bag and pulled out a long barrel six-shooter and tucked it into his belt. He pulled a box of ammunition and an oiled rag from the same bag and put them in a button-up pocket on the side of his pants.

He listened for any sounds of humans but heard none. He placed a pair of sunglasses on the beak of his nose and began to work his way through sage and rabbit brush and across a flat, open area near the river. From there, he stayed close to high cliffs at the canyon's edge, where Harold and the crew were more likely to look for a secluded place to camp. The popular place to camp was at the beach, just out of sight and downriver.

Paul had no illusions about what it would be like working for Boss. The man was not flashy or brilliant, but he could be brutal and was certainly not stupid. Boss had quietly built a financial empire and, unlike most people with wealth, kept it well hidden. He would stop at little to keep it safely in his hands. Paul was lucky to get this break. If Boss needed more help, Harold was his ticket in. But Boss had no clue what Paul was really up to.

Paul stopped and scanned the area, listening. Farther to his right, the cliff dipped south and into shadow. There appeared to be a gentle overhang. He moved carefully along.

Boss was not a young guy, he thought. With the

success he's had in antiquities, and the occasional drug deliveries from Mexico, he ought to be close to retirement. Maybe Boss would be turning the work over to Harold soon, or to Boss's nephew, Bobby.

Suddenly, a rancid smell ripped him from his thoughts. Death. Something was very dead under the rock overhang. He looked up and saw a gang of buzzards circling the high cliff, confirming the news.

He pulled his gun instinctively and moved closer to the smell. A green T-shirt hung from the bushes, maybe there to dry in the sun. There, on the ground below it, were two bodies. Shit.

He scanned the area again. Seeing nothing, he moved closer to the body nearest him. Damn it. Harold.

He moved to the other body. Trevor. He'd met him once at the Wagon Wheel Bar with Harold. Instinctively, he took two pictures with his cell phone, one of Harold, one of Trevor. He lingered a moment, staring at their bodies. He'd seen corpses before, but not shot neatly in the forehead, undoubtedly in their sleep.

Think, goddamn it. He had a five alarm fire going on here, an honest to shit life or death emergency.

Where the hell was Bobby?

CHAPTER 54

The roar of whitewater drowned out all other sounds of life, even Ethan's own breathing. He watched with a sense of awe as Anya powered her boat to the left, deftly guiding it as she watched the rapids on their right.

Ethan followed her move, paddling to line up with the left shore, then rowing toward it.

In mere moments, a huge rock appeared on their right, the river bellowing over it like a jet engine. Water reared high above the rock, spraying whitecaps into the air, plunging into a crater of water below, swirling and rising and collapsing on itself as it went. He could feel the waves rocking his raft even several yards away. As quickly as the sound had engulfed him, it started to fade.

"Ethan!" Anya yelled across, her voice a mere reminder among the sound of throbbing rapids to look up, pay attention.

He saw her rowing toward the right shore. Quickly, he spun the raft so his back was to the same shore and began to row.

The current was much faster here than in the stretch of flat water he'd gotten used to. He could hear and sense the rapids directly in front of him. He dipped the oars and pulled mightily with mediocre results. He forced himself to row faster and harder, desperate to avoid the coming whitewater.

The sound of the first rapid he'd passed was nothing compared to the vibration and roar of the waves ahead. All he could do was keep rowing, putting his legs into it, straining his back against the oars.

Without warning, the front of his raft dipped sideways into a trough, nearly tossing him out of the boat. His upriver oar swung through thin air, angled out of the water. He leveled out for a moment, bracing himself, then the raft buckled inward as it crashed into a wave ten feet above his head. His fingers slipped from the oars and found brief purchase on the center frame. The river pounded him like a waterfall and he lost all sense of direction as the raft spun high on the cresting water, spray blasting his skin like shotgun pellets.

The raft slid sideways across the downriver slope of the high wave. He was weightless for a moment as it fell toward another trough and then, at the bottom, the raft buckled again, tossing him clear of the boat like a piece of cork.

He had time for only half a breath before the cold water sucked him under, spinning him down through the roiling currents. He struggled for a second, flailing his arms and legs, then stopped. As water pressure began to hurt his ears, he knew he was too deep to swim up, that he'd use his air too quickly if he tried to fight the current. Let the life jacket do its job, he thought, if it can. He forced himself to relax, to conserve his energy, to let the river take him where it would. To do that, he had to surrender - fully, unconditionally – to the power of the water, the flow of rain, snowmelt, and desert springs all merged into one gargantuan muscle of river tearing through bedrock itself, carving grand canyons out of solid stone. What could anyone do against that?

His arms and legs tingled painfully then went numb - from the cold or lack of oxygen he could not tell. His mind flashed to Relic's water bottle. Water, the one thing he could not live without in this harsh and beautiful desert; the one thing that would now kill him. He would never take water for granted again.

Though his eyes were closed, stars and spears of light flashed across them. He spun more slowly than before but disorientation had seized control. Was he right side up? Rising? Sinking?

His chest burned like molten magma, cooking and crackling, dying for a simple gasp of air to release the flame. His muscles moved involuntarily to expel his breath but he forced them back. He knew he had to breathe, and soon, even if it meant sucking his lungs full of water, but he rallied back against the thought, squeezing it out, willing himself to never breathe again. When his throat convulsed, the world became a void.

CHAPTER 55

Paul walked slowly away from the bodies. Up canyon was the dig site. According to Boss, Bobby had found it last winter. The main canyon rose on the southern end and a smaller one wound its way to the north. The popular camping spot for whitewater rafters was to his left, a bit north, by the tall cottonwood trees.

He worked his way along, seeing no obvious footprints or other recent signs of human activity. He avoided the cottonwoods and scrambled over boulders in some places until he passed the main trail that went up the southern canyon to the old moonshiner's still. He kept moving until he reached a narrow trail where the side canyon opened.

He stood there for a moment to rest. Who could have killed Harold and Trevor? Left their bodies for the buzzards? If a tourist group had come by here, they would not have camped anywhere near Harold. They would have camped under the cottonwoods. There was no need for them to come into contact at all. And why would one of them kill Harold and Trevor, anyway?

He pictured it again, the position of their bodies, face up, atop of the ground cloths and down-filled bags. They hadn't seen it coming.

Where are you Bobby?

Paul took a deep breath and continued up the trail, stopping frequently to look and listen. The path wound upward steeply for a bit, then leveled across an open area. Gentle switchbacks took him another fifty feet or so higher. The ground became sandy here as he walked around a large, truck-sized boulder. Shelves of sandstone appeared on his left. He followed open ground back to the trail then curved around a group of boulders to an open area straight ahead.

That smell hit him again. A square shaped pit lay about fifty yards away and he knew what he would find. He walked slowly to the edge of the hole and saw what was left of the body, after the buzzards and maybe even a coyote had been at it. It was a man, but did not look like Bobby. He was too heavy. Something about him looked older too.

Who the hell is killing people in this canyon?

Paul took a quick photo with his phone. The hole was squared off and even-sided. This must be the site Boss had sent Harold and Bobby to dig, so he decided to keep following the trail higher up the canyon.

A lone crow watched solemnly from the ridge.

CHAPTER 56

Ethan's face smashed tight against a hard, white surface, his arms pinned high above him, lungs desperately sucking deeper breaths. Consciousness returned slowly to him, in ever larger circles, as he hung suspended from the drifting raft. He heard sounds, a woman's voice, calling him softly from above. He slowed his breathing a bit and wiggled his feet in the water.

"Relax and breathe," Anya repeated, holding his arms as they draped across the raft. "We're out of the rapids now, just catch your breath. No hurry."

The raft circled slowly in a back water current by the shore. He noticed high trees come in and out of view and hugged the raft to his cheek.

After two full minutes, Ethan looked up at Anya and nodded.

"Just stay there, I'll get us to the river bank. Can

you hold on?"

He grabbed the safety rope that circled the raft and nodded.

Anya let go of his arms and moved back to the oars. With a couple of strong pulls, the boat slid onto sand. Carter pulled his hair behind his ears and waded quickly to Ethan.

"Give me your hand."

Ethan took a moment, then slid his right hand off the rope. Carter grabbed his arm and slowly led Ethan toward shore.

Ethan's legs and arms felt like stones tied loosely to his torso. With tremendous effort, he followed Carter to a shady spot in the sand beneath a box elder tree and sat.

"Man, we thought you were a goner there, buddy. We saw your raft, but no Ethan in it, you know what I mean?"

Ethan took measured breaths. "Thank you."

"Anya got your raft, it came in ahead of you. Man, I figured you were way downriver by now. We ran down but couldn't find you anywhere."

Anya anchored the raft and hurried over to them. She sat next to Ethan. "Are you OK?" She put her arm on his shoulder.

"Don't know yet. I'm really weak."

"You had a very close call. Your body is close to shock. You should lie down for as long as you need to. We're not going anywhere. We'll camp here for the night."

Ethan nodded. Carter stared at him like a museum curiosity then looked to Anya. She cleared her throat.

"Carter, would you help me start unloading the boats?"

"Sure."

"Would you start with the kitchen table and gear?" She pointed. "I'll be right over."

Carter glanced again at Ethan, then stood and went to the rafts. He reported to the others that Ethan was all right but needed time to rest. Carter began lifting what he could, careful not to over use his ailing wrist.

Anya turned toward Ethan.

"Sorry I didn't make it through those rapids," he said. "I nearly lost the raft…"

"Oh my god, do not apologize. I feel horrible. I thought you would be fine, and you almost didn't make it back to shore. Ever." She took another breath. "I'm the one who put you in that danger, it's my responsibility, and I'm so, so very… very sorry." Anya broke into a sob and covered her face in her hands.

Ethan put his arm around her and let her cry. He was too exhausted to say more.

CHAPTER 57

Paul took a deep swallow of water and trudged higher up the trail. He crossed a crescent-shaped flat and moved through rocky debris as the trail faded farther into the landscape. He could see the canyon turn sharply to his left, which likely meant there was no place to go after that. Sweating, he picked his way over brush and scree to reach the curve, where it opened again. He went toward a large boulder on his left, noticing that the area was sandy. A small seep of water nourished desert ferns straight ahead of him on the canyon wall.

Then, he noticed that same smell again and pinched his nose shut. He walked around the large rock and there, on the sand to his right, lay what was left of Bobby.

Bobby had been shot in the head. Paul stared at the ugly bullet hole, a funnel of blood smeared past his hair and over the dry ground in an oily shade of maroon.

Footprints circled the body but there appeared to be no way to get farther up the canyon. Paul searched the area and found only a worn, green cap with some kind of logo on the front. Whoever did this killed Harold and Trevor in their sleep and probably chased Bobby up here to kill him too. Why kill them? To take over the dig site? To steal what they'd found? He grabbed and twisted the hat in frustration. Abruptly, he remembered the logo: it belonged to an outfit that ran rafters through the canyons. Maybe one of them had a reason he hadn't considered. And whoever did it is still in play.

It suddenly felt like the canyon had a thousand eyes, peering from black cracks and shaded ledges circling above his head. He needed to get out of here, and fast. The killer is either right here with him, watching and waiting, or somewhere downriver. Either way, Boss will want answers. Paul wanted answers, too. He pulled out his cell phone and took a picture of what was left of Bobby.

It's time to bring some justice to this sonofabitch. More nervous than angry, Paul began to trot back down the trail.

CHAPTER 58

"Feeling any better?" Norma asked.

Ethan moved up to the serving table. "Much better, thanks. I sure needed to rest though…"

"We were pretty worried about you for a while."

"It all happened so fast. One second I was in my raft, rowing as hard as I could, the next I was hanging onto Anya's raft."

"Potatoes?" She held a spoon toward his plate.

"Sure."

Norma lowered her voice. "Anya was under some serious stress over you."

"I was under some serious stress myself." He looked up from his food and then caught Norma's meaning. "Oh, yes, of course."

She nodded. "Corn?"

"Yes, thanks." He stood there for a moment. "I

should talk to her some more?"

"Exactly." Norma smiled. She glanced about and called, "Next?"

Ethan took some ground beef from the grill and found a chair. The food was wonderful, but his stomach had not completely unclenched. He wanted to eat more, but only finished half.

Carter pulled up a chair nearby and began to wolf down his food. Anya sat in the sand by the propane stove.

Norma's niece busied herself with a sketch pad, checking the nearest cliffs across the river, then returning intently to her pencil and paper. Ethan wondered what ever happened to her electronic gadget.

Darren and Millie approached Ethan carefully, watching their steps, holding plates of food.

"That was really something you did, running those rapids," he said, shifting his feet. Millie watched Darren with a wry grin, like a little girl who knew a secret.

These two are a little odd, even unnerving, Ethan thought. "Yes, well, I'd prefer to stay *in* the boat next time."

"Of course, of course. But you got back to shore OK, that's what counts."

"Well, and Anya snared my raft while I was swimming."

"It came right in to us." Darren waved his hand toward the river. "We were on shore and Anya stayed in our boat. Yours was floating over. We could see you weren't on it, so Anya pushed it closer toward shore then rowed out with our raft to find you."

"My raft just floated on in?"

"Pretty much. Carter swam out a bit, into the backwater, and grabbed the rope on the side, then swam back till we could wade out and pull it the rest of the way in."

"We were lucky then. My raft has all the food and cooking stuff."

"Everything *plus* the kitchen sink," Darren said. Millie smiled at his joke. "We just wanted to say we're glad you're safe and sound."

"Thanks."

The couple glanced at each other with what seemed like a fleeting nervousness, nodded, then wandered toward a large, worn tree trunk that had washed ashore. They sat on the driftwood and ate quietly.

Ethan pictured Lars in his brightly colored shirt. He wanted to talk with him, ask him how his life was going, and where it was going, and why he was working so damn hard he could barely enjoy any of it. Lars had seemed to enjoy himself out here, though. At least while he could.

Across the river, the canyon folded open like a huge picture book, its glossy pages stretching into the distance. Red-faced cliffs faded into shades of coral and cream as the expansive country blended into the evening sky.

Ethan was surprised by how low late it had gotten. It seemed only moments ago that he'd been rowing with every muscle in his body, rolling with the crashing waves. Holding onto his life with only a breath. He was still tense and exhausted.

He set his plate on the ground and opened a can of soda. The carbonation burned its way down his throat, making him cough.

CHAPTER 59

Paul knew he was chancing it, running down the trail like this, knowing he could pull a muscle or even fall, but on balance it seemed the best he could do. Every few hundred yards, he stopped suddenly at a convenient rock or brush. He knelt and listened intently for any sound, any noise at all that might be made by man. He heard none.

Knowing an ambush could lie at the next corner, Paul scouted the ledges and likely places to hide, then stood and jogged down the trail again, not sure if the last sound he would hear would be a rifle, or whether he'd hear it at all before he was dead. But the alternative was imponderable: leaving the trail meant painstaking progress over and around boulders and ledges above the drainage. If the killer was downriver, leaving the trail would take far too much time - Paul could never catch up with someone who'd already left the canyon. And if the killer was still nearby, leaving the trail still might not save him from attack. This little side canyon was perfect for a surprise assault.

He kept up his pace for over an hour, until he reached the bottom, where the terrain leveled out. An evening sun lay low on the sandstone rim across the river, painting long, dark shadows behind the trees and clumps of crested wheat grass. Small trails wound through an area where campers liked to stay, just above the beach. He walked briskly, catching his breath as he went. Still no sign of anyone else.

Paul reached his kayak and pulled the pistol from his waist. He climbed in and set the revolver on his legs, within easy reach. He drank from his water bottle, snapped on his helmet, and paddled up the gentle back-water, above the blue rafts left hidden by Harold's crew. Seeing no worrisome signs, he wrapped his pistol back in its oilcloth and into the purple dry bag and clipped it to the webbing inside the kayak.

He'd spent nearly all day hiking up the canyon and back. It was getting late and he had a decision to make: stay here or go down river. If the killer was still in the canyon, Paul could lie in wait for him. If the killer was gone, well, he could still wait for him to return to the dig site, but that could take days. The closest cell phone service was downriver at the take-out spot. He should tell Boss what he'd found as soon as he could so a new team could get back to the dig, this time with some real firepower. And if the killer has left the canyon, who knew what treasures he's already taken with him? Paul could always return to the dig site later. But if he could catch the bastard now, while the trail might still be warm...

He gathered his energy and paddled hard across the river at a ninety degree angle. The flow carried him past the light blue rafts again, past the tall brush, and toward the cottonwoods. By the time he was across from the trees, he'd paddled nearly half way across the river, heading for the opposite shore. Soon, he was past the cottonwoods and a Puebloan ruin along the base of the cliff. In a few more minutes, he was across the main current, watching for a landing on the other shore.

An hour later, he found a low opening in a stand of dense tamarisk. He slid out of the kayak and pulled the boat high onto shore, hidden from anyone else who might float past. Exhausted, he lay there for a while before setting up a quick camp for the night.

Tomorrow would come early, well before sunrise. He had rapids to run at first light, canyons to scout, and a killer to find.

CHAPTER 60

Golden grass waved in the breeze the way flames sway in a camp fire. In the distance, tower walls glowed with the dying heat of the sun - solid, anchored, chunks of bedrock laid bare by the millennia. Time was but a ghost. Ethan just stared, like he was seeing the planet Earth for the very first time.

He heard someone come up behind him and set up a camp chair next to his. Carter said nothing for a while, enjoying the setting sun in silence, the way it should be.

When the light finally retreated over the canyon rim, Carter looked over at Ethan.

"You OK, man?" His voice was serious, concerned.

"Yes. No."

Carter nodded.

"Maybe."

"You look tense, like you're all tied up or

something."

"Yes." It was all he could think of to say.

Carter lit a half-used joint and took a long, deep drag while Ethan watched. Carter reached over, offering to share. What the hell, Ethan thought. He took the joint, sucked some of the smoke into his lungs, then coughed it back out.

"Thanks."

"No sweat. Glad to have someone to smoke it with."

"I don't smoke pot." Ethan felt embarrassed as soon as he said it. "That sounds judgmental. I don't mean it that way."

"We're cool."

"You're cool. Thanks."

"Try one more hit. You didn't get enough to notice anything on that last one."

Ethan smiled then took a deeper pull of it into his lungs. He managed not to cough this time and released it slowly.

"Better?"

"Thanks."

They sat quietly for a while. The sky melted from deep blue to starry black. To their left, Anya had started a campfire. Friendly chatter floated to them with the breeze.

Slowly, the muscles in Ethan's neck began to relax. He stretched low to the ground and popped his back into place.

"Hey, I think I figured out what's up with Millie and Darren," Carter squinted and flicked the ashes from his joint.

"Oh?"

"You know, they've been a little weird this whole time…"

Ethan nodded.

"Millie told me they were mugged the week before they came on this trip."

"Really?"

"Yeah, a guy pulled a gun on them and everything and they got away. Ran down the street, worried they'd get shot in the back."

Ethan stiffened.

"I mean, Jesus. She's had nightmares about it," Carter said.

"I'm sure."

"Now everything that's happened on this trip, it kinda freaked her out."

Ethan looked around but could not see Millie or Darren.

"But I think she felt better telling me about it. Least, I hope so."

"Yeah, well, that's good." Ethan remembered how suspicious Carter had been about the couple and regretted his own concerns.

"Another hit?" Carter asked.

"No, my friend, but thank you."

Then Ethan remembered Norma's hint, and something else he did not want to regret. "I need to talk with Anya for a minute, if you don't mind." He stood and folded his chair.

"I think I'll join the others now… enjoy the campfire for a while," Carter said, gathering his things. "See you later."

"Later." Ethan walked toward the firelight and waved for Anya to step away with him. She nodded and went to intercept him.

"Sit with me for a minute?" he asked.

"Of course." Anya motioned toward the raft, away from the rest of the group. Ethan leaned his chair on the ground and sat next to her on the rubber tubing.

"How are you?" he asked.

"All right, I guess."

"No, really, how are you doing?"

"I'm still processing it all. You could have drowned out there."

"But I didn't. I'm alive and well."

"You're making light of it, and that's understandable. But I thought we'd lost you. It's hard enough losing Lars, then finding out who Tim really was. Now, he's dead too. This trip is a total fucking nightmare and I'm in charge of it all." Her voice cracked.

"It's not your fault, Anya."

"No, now I'm making it about me. I don't mean to. It's not about me, Ethan." Quiet engulfed them. Forty yards away, Norma added driftwood to the fire, brightening the flames.

Anya wiped her eyes and sniffled. "Tim seemed like such a perfectly nice guy. He was a really good guide too. He knew the canyons, the birds, the vegetation, the history. I didn't know him very well, but, really, it's a horrible betrayal. Of the group, of us, of me. I'm as angry as I've ever been in my life and as sad as I've ever been, all at the same time. He was a rat bastard and he murdered 'in cold blood,' as they say. And poor Lars dead... a good, kind, hard-working guy who just wanted some time away from the grind. I want to scream until I've lost my voice."

"I couldn't say it any better than that," Ethan whispered. He thought about how Tim had fooled them all. And he remembered how eerie it felt pulling Tim's limp body across the dirt, sensing ghostly movement in the dead. They sat in silence for a while.

"I nearly lost you to the rapids," Anya said. "My own stupidity, my own fault putting you out there so early, with so little experience."

"I made the choice to go," he said firmly. "And I made the choice to get the hell out of my tiny, little self-absorbed life too. Stop listening to my mind-numbing roommate. Get the hell out of that dungeon. I did that, my choice." He pointed to his chest. "My choice."

"I see," she nodded. "I respect that, Ethan."

He filled his lungs. "You forget how valuable a simple breath of air really is, 'till it's beyond you." They held each other's gaze. "Really, really, valuable." He suddenly found his own words funny, in sound and in meaning. His body felt weightless. He grinned broadly and reached for her hand and Anya welcomed it, squeezing tightly, returning his smile.

"This is funny?" she asked with a chuckle.

"Fucking hilarious," Ethan replied, laughing with her, holding her warm hand in the dark, hearing muted voices by the fire and an ancient counsel from the ever flowing river.

CHAPTER 61

Ethan woke, propped himself on his elbows, and looked around. Everyone else seemed sound asleep. The rafts rocked gently in the lapping water. Sunshine teased brighter shades of rose from high sandstone along one side of the canyon.

He put on his hat, wiggled out of the sleeping bag, and stretched. He stood and walked quietly to one of the food containers and found a raisin bagel and plastic bottle of orange juice. He made his way along a narrow trail leading away from the river and looked for a good place to sit.

The path led upward and through an open area, still in shadow in the early hour. From there, the trail seemed to peter out, but a jumble of rocks close to the cliffs looked inviting. Two large towers of dark stone rose from level ground like the thumbs of a giant. He wandered to a chair-sized stone between them and sat.

He had a clear view of the river rolling through the massive canyon and the backwater current churning along the sandy shore. From here, the rafts were the size of jigsaw pieces. The kitchen table and gear stretched nearby. Millie's and Darren's tent was pitched in tall grass maybe fifty yards from the common area. No one seemed to be stirring.

Sunlight began to flood the opposite side of the canyon, sliding down the sheer walls in a line – a gauge of the planet's rotation, a barometer of time. He shivered in the cool shade, wishing he'd brought a jacket.

He tore the bagel in half and ate it in large bites, washing it down with cold juice. In a few minutes his belly was full. He squashed the empty plastic bottle flat and tucked it into his pants pocket. He took a deep breath and watched the morning age as light began to hit their little camp.

The world was sublimely quiet.

He saw movement near the boats. Anya was moving things to the stove area, probably getting ready to cook breakfast. His face flushed warmly when he thought of last night, how they'd held hands and talked, how she'd shown him the North Star, Venus, the Orion constellation. He'd tried to stay in those moments but was so tired he finally had to say good night and collapse.

In the distance, something the size and shape of a toothpick moved briskly across the wide river toward camp.

A kayak.

CHAPTER 62

Relic moved steadily along the plateau while the air was cool, the sun still low on the horizon behind him. Yesterday, he'd watched for traffic along the river at Horse Canyon. A man had hurried down the trail to a kayak he'd hidden in the grass. Suspicious, Relic had decided to hike out of Horse Canyon, up the old Hopi trail, and travel downriver, too. He'd started his cross country trek before sunrise.

He pulled the straps on his daypack tighter and picked his way around a batch of cactus. As he walked across the upper plateau, the next large canyon downstream from Horse Canyon began to take shape, a left-tilted "U" with a wiggle in the middle. The abyss yawned deeper before him as he approached the edge of the cliffs. From there, he searched for the cairn he'd stacked two seasons ago, marking the place to descend.

After wandering along the edge for a while, he spotted the stack of balanced rocks and strode to the lip of a narrow crevasse a few feet away. He gazed across the expanse at a band of sunlight as it dipped onto the far side of the canyon walls. Still in the shade, the river below shouldered its way through dark red rocks, cutting a swath through eons of desert stone.

The floodplain was wider and lower to the river here, leaving plenty of room for an old outlaw cabin and horse corrals on the upstream side. He searched the shoreline with binoculars until he found two white rafts near a stand of box elders at the downstream end of the canyon. If he was right about the man in the kayak back at Horse Canyon, he would be stopping here too.

Relic reached for his water and took a swig, then replaced it in his pack. Gingerly, he moved to the edge of the cliff and sat, then wiggled his right foot down to a three inch toe-hold and began to descend.

CHAPTER 63

Paul had left his bivouac early and run Black Heart rapids in good time. Now in calmer water, he stopped paddling when rafts came into view on the right shoreline. He knew from a symbol on the near-side raft that the site was camp for a whitewater touring group. As he drifted closer, he recognized the same logo he'd seen on the baseball cap near Bobby's body. He floated for a moment or two, decided on a bold plan of action, and paddled straight for the boats.

In a few moments, he was on the beach on the upriver side of the little canyon, slipping his paddle into its Velcro straps. A tall, pretty young woman waved hello. Two tents were at the camp, one near the sandy beach, the other farther away. He could see what looked like sleeping bags by the water. The woman was moving pans onto a grill and arranging a table.

Paul reached deep into his kayak and slid a wallet-sized fold of leather from a pouch. He pulled himself from the boat and slid his revolver into a special holster on the belt at the back of his pants, under his shirt. He removed his whitewater helmet and dropped it in the kayak. He stood slowly and readied himself. This had almost certainly been the group that was in Horse Canyon a day or two earlier and he had a feeling they knew about the killings there. He began a relaxed, deliberate walk toward the group.

Anya's friendly smile took him off guard. She hardly seemed like someone in hiding, or on the run. He walked down the shore- line, trying to be casual. Someone was stirring in the nearby tent. A young man with long, dark hair sat on the grass, scratching his head. He gave Paul a quick wave. Paul nodded back.

Paul walked past two empty sleeping bags. He knew the habit of whitewater guides to sleep on their boats. By rough calculation, that meant probably two campers in each tent, plus two sleeping on the beach, plus one for each raft. Eight people? Maybe one or two more.

"Good morning," Anya spoke loudly. "What a beautiful day to be on the river."

"Good morning," Paul said, walking up to her. "Yes, a beautiful day to be on the river." He looked up and down the beach.

"Coffee?" Anya offered.

"Sure." Paul looked at the camp kitchen.

"Mugs over there." She pointed. "Coffee pot on the stove. Use the oven mitt on the table, the pot is hot."

Paul accepted the courtesy with a quick nod. He busied himself with the coffee, adding sugar and canned milk to the mug and took a cautious sip. Anya added water to the pancake mix and stirred.

"Where are my manners?" Paul smiled. "Let me introduce myself. I'm Officer Paul Strauss, National Park Service." He flipped open the leather case and flashed a badge.

Anya's eyes widened. "My name is Anya. I'm the guide on this whitewater trip."

Paul put his badge away and nodded. She'd said "the" guide, singular. But there were two boats.

"Well, I'm going to need your help, Anna." He sipped his coffee.

"Anya."

"Anya. I've been up Horse Canyon. Yesterday. You know what I found?"

Anya's mouth went dry. "Yes, unfortunately, I do."

Paul watched her carefully. "We need to talk about that. I need to talk to everyone here about that."

"Of course." Anya set the mixing bowl down and took a breath. "You're out of uniform, Officer Strauss."

"I'm undercover, Anya."

They stared at each other for a moment. Paul casually pulled the revolver from his pants and inspected the cylinder. "That's not going to be an issue, is it?" He observed her from beneath his brow.

Anya stared at the gun. Paul casually passed its aim toward her stomach, then re-holstered it.

"Of course not, officer." Anya said, holding his gaze. "I'm hoping you'll join us for breakfast," she said without a smile.

CHAPTER 64

Ethan watched a stranger make his way toward the camp kitchen, scanning the area as he went. Ethan could see the lanky man and Anya speaking, but could not make out their words. For a quick second, the man extended what looked like a gun toward Anya's midriff, then tucked it quickly behind his back.

Did Ethan imagine it? Had it really happened? He blinked. Anya moved stiffly behind the propane stove, appearing tense, uncertain. She and the stranger seemed to be talking again.

Ethan had to get closer to them, close enough to hear what was going on.

He slid off the rock and looked around carefully. If he went back to the little trail, he'd be out in the open. He could make his way along the canyon wall on the downstream side and stay in the morning shadows. There were plenty of couch-sized rocks to hide behind.

He suddenly felt vulnerable, impotent. A rush of fear and adrenaline made him lightheaded.

He found two fist shaped rocks and crammed them into his pockets. It was pathetic, really, but it felt better than nothing at all.

CHAPTER 65

Paul put a pleasant smile on his face and pulled up a chair by the kitchen. As long as the guide cooperated, the group was likely to go along. Someone would either tell him the truth, or reveal it by accident.

Anya announced that breakfast was ready and Carter, Norma, and Lisa shuffled over. Anya introduced Paul as an undercover federal officer investigating the deaths in Horse Canyon. Whatever joy might have blossomed under the deep blue sky was quashed. Carter seemed especially nervous, eating slowly and in silence, off by himself.

"Go ahead and eat, while it's hot," Paul said, eyeing Anya. He wanted everyone out of their tents and the chance to watch their reactions to Officer Paul Strauss.

After a short while, Millie and Darren arrived. They got the same news and shared the same muted response.

As they began to eat, the others finished. No one asked for second helpings. Norma gave most of her breakfast to her niece, Lisa.

Paul stood ceremoniously and cleared his throat. Everyone turned their attention to him.

"I need information, and your cooperation. This is a federal investigation now, and refusal to cooperate is a federal crime. It's my job to find who killed those people in Horse Canyon and bring them to justice." He nodded solemnly.

He saw Anya watching him carefully. She was not just the guide by job title; these people would follow her wherever she led. And she was sharp. Paul would have to keep a tight rein on her.

Paul turned toward Anya. He would gauge her honesty by her reactions to his questions but also by the reactions of the others. If she lied, someone would react, someone would reveal it.

"What are the names of everyone here?"

They each introduced themselves.

"Is there any member of this group not here with us, right now?"

Anya looked at her feet for a moment, then answered Paul directly. "Tim Johnson was the other guide for this trip. He is one of the ones who died in that canyon."

Tim? Paul had only seen Boss's crew and a large man dead at the dig site. "Describe him."

Anya did so. Tim was not the man in the pit. Paul thought for a moment. "I found no one in that canyon that fit that description." It was a statement, and an accusation.

"I don't know what you found, but Lars and Tim were killed up there," Anya replied.

Paul nodded. Lars must have been the one he'd seen in at the dig site.

"Whose sleeping bag is that," Paul pointed, "on the beach?"

Carter almost answered.

"Ethan's," Anya said.

"Where is Ethan now?"

"I don't know. He was here last night. When I got up this morning, his bag was empty. He didn't come for breakfast, as you can see."

Norma and Millie looked at each other. "He almost drowned yesterday," Norma said.

Paul turned toward her. "How did that happen?"

"He was on the raft," Norma pointed, "but he's new at it. He's never rafted before, but we needed someone to do it."

"Tim died in that canyon," Anya added. "Ethan volunteered to take his place on one of the rafts. So, Ethan took the supply raft and I took the passenger raft."

"I did not find anyone matching Tim's description in that canyon," Paul said.

"Ethan found out that Tim had killed Lars. Lars was one of our guests," she said, looking toward her feet. Lars's death still felt like her responsibility. "Tim chased Ethan into the cliffs, and Tim fell up there and died. Ethan came down from the canyon alone, and he saved my life."

Millie looked at Darren. "Ethan was not with us on this trip, originally," he said.

Anya's eyes narrowed at Darren, her face expressing a sense of betrayal.

"What does that mean?" Paul asked.

"He had an accident on a mountain bike and hiked down into the canyon for help. We let him join the group," Darren explained.

Paul had heard enough. "Someone is either lying to me about a guy named Tim, who is somewhere right here, in this canyon, or lying about this Ethan guy. Maybe Ethan has fooled all of you, killed Tim and the others and just walked out of Horse Canyon."

Anya shook her head.

"Falling to your death seems like a pretty amateur move for an experienced canyon guide. If there *is* a guy named Ethan on this trip, he's your killer."

"No way, that's not it," Carter stood.

"Shut up." Paul raised an open palm toward Carter.

Norma and Lisa sat up straighter and looked at each other.

"You," Paul pointed to Anya, "are going to cooperate with this investigation or spend time in prison for obstruction of justice. We are going to go for a short walk." He pulled his pistol.

"Officer!" Norma called.

"I'm going to find out who did these killings and I'm going to find out now." With his gun, he motioned for Anya to leave the kitchen and start up the trail.

"Stay put, you understand?" he said to the group. Darren nodded. Carter stared. "You are all under arrest. You are all ordered to stay here in camp."

Norma's expression turned dark. Lisa's eyes went wide.

"And just to make sure…" Paul fired two rounds in quick succession. The sound echoed through the canyon.

CHAPTER 66

Relic had worked his way down the narrow crevasse to a ledge on his left. He'd flattened himself to the sandstone wall and begun a traverse when he heard two distinct pistol shots, down toward the tree line. He froze for a moment, listening to the metallic sound fade, then resumed his sideways shuffle to a wider ledge. From there, he took a long switch-back route down toward a tall cone of rough scree. He stopped to look for movement near the campsite, but noticed none.

The slope before him led to a large rock-slide along the downstream side of the canyon, tucked away from the river. He headed there as fast as his tired legs could carry him, hoping not to find more dead bodies down below.

****

Ethan jumped at the twin percussions. The bangs repeated in deeper tones as they bounced off the sheer, red walls.

He'd worked his way close to the camp, but stayed hidden behind a group of boulders. He was still in the shade, the sun marching closer to him every minute.

He raised his head and looked again toward the little group. Norma had her hands over her mouth. Lisa was gripping Norma's arm. Carter, Millie and Darren all looked shell-shocked. Had the stranger shot someone? Where was he? Where was Anya?

A chilling fear rushed into him and he shivered. Just like in Horse Canyon, he thought, when Bobby shot and chased him through the dark of night, he was weaponless, absolutely defenseless. And this time, he couldn't just run away.

Minutes stretched into the morning air. A lone crow circled an updraft along the canyon walls, its hoarse voice calling at something. He sensed motion to his left. There, Anya walked about three yards in front of the man, who had his pistol aimed at her back. Ethan ducked behind some sage brush and moved slowly away from them.

"Call him."

Anya stopped and took a breath. "Ethan?"

"Louder."

"Ethan!"

"Move ahead. Keep going till I tell you to stop."

Anya walked gingerly across a sandy area and past the high thumbs of sandstone where Ethan had eaten his bagel. They were in shadow for a moment, then back into the light. Paul followed closely behind her. She wound her way toward the river and around a bend in the tall, walnut-colored cliffs.

Ethan circled below them, moving with them toward the river. He pulled himself onto the edge of a large bench of rock above the current. If he could get Anya into the same position, they could jump a few feet back down behind the rock and into the swirling water. He could hear them coming around the bend.

Anya came around the corner and stopped. Her eyes locked with Ethan's.

His knees weakened and his feet felt anchored to a cushion in motion, like he was standing on a water bed. He tried to straighten on the swaying mattress.

Paul slid behind Anya, to her right. They stood about thirty yards away.

"Well, there he is, flesh and blood after all," Paul said.

"Ethan," Anya's voice cracked.

"Ethan, I am Officer Paul Strauss."

A police officer? Could it be? Could he really just explain his way out of this? The thought tempted him like nothing before ever had. But what about the gun shots he'd heard?

"I am here investigating the murders of three people in Horse Canyon and the disappearance of one other. Well... plus a man named Tim, unless that's really you. If there was such a person, there are two missing."

Ethan shifted closer to the ledge behind him.

"You are under arrest on suspicion of murder," Paul said. "Put your hands above your head and get down on your knees."

Anya's eyes were filled with worry.

The only words that came to Ethan's mind were a Hollywood cliché. "Let me see some I.D.," he said with more authority than he felt.

Paul held up something the size and color of a police badge then tucked it away.

"Throw it over here, so I can see it," Ethan leaned forward.

"Enough of this bullshit." Paul pushed Anya ahead of him as they moved closer to Ethan. "I want to know what you're doing digging around in that canyon. What have you found?"

"Nothing." Ethan circled slowly to his right, hoping to give Anya a clear pathway to the ledge, but the sandstone dropped quickly behind him. Any farther and he'd have to jump over the edge into the water.

"You shot Harold and Trevor in cold blood, in their sleep, you bastard!" Paul spat. He raised the gun toward Ethan.

"You're nuts! I haven't killed anybody." Ethan raised his hands.

"What did you find up there?" Paul's eyes narrowed to tiny beads of blue. "What kind of artifacts? Sandals? Bows and arrows? What?"

"Wait, wait," Anya raised her hands and turned toward Paul, partially blocking his view of Ethan.

Paul raised the gun to Anya's head.

"Whoa, whoa, whoa," Ethan moved his open hands toward the ground. "Officer, hold on. There's no problem here, see? I'm not armed. I just want to know what's going on then I'll go with you. Quietly. Without trouble."

Paul's lip curled in a grin. He stepped to the side of Anya so he could see them both.

"Just tell me what I'm being arrested for." Ethan's eyes searched Anya's. "No problems."

Paul stared at Ethan and seemed to relax just a little.

Almost imperceptibly, Anya shook her head at Ethan. Something was seriously wrong, and it wasn't just his impending arrest.

CHAPTER 67

Relic heard voices up ahead; one sounded like Ethan's. He'd damn near sprained his left ankle on the trot down here and needed to stop, but feared he could not. He pressed on past the huge tumble of stones that made up the rock fall, out across a wide flat, then past a pair of high columns of blood-red sandstone.

The voices grew louder as he approached. He tried to catch his breath as he moved from boulder to boulder. He had a glimpse of the back of a man's head and a woman with long, brown hair. The man had a pistol aimed at her ear.

Damn it, this whole fucking thing was way out of control. Those looters in Horse Canyon must have found something really important, worth a mountain of money, and he feared what it must be. He touched the Mexica head-piece in his pocket; he'd not had time to rebury it.

He kneeled to the ground and removed his day-pack. What he wouldn't give to have his Colt revolver right now. But that was far away, hidden at a camp in another district. He pulled his sling shot out and put the day pack back on. For now, and yet again, this would have to do.

Relic put several quarter-sized stones in his pocket and one into the sling. Then he slowly stood just above the edge of the rock he was behind. The man was shouting something. Ethan was saying "no, no." He straightened his left arm, locking the elbow then pulled back on the sling.

Ethan's fists clenched, then opened again. Anya's dark eyes widened.

Paul seemed to notice how close Ethan was to the ledge and moved to Anya's side. Relic adjusted his aim.

Ethan flexed his knees, balancing with his hands out to his sides.

Accounting for his tendency to aim too far left, Relic released the stone to the right of the man's head. The rock hit him dead center just above his neck.

Ethan leapt at that same moment, screaming, smashing awkwardly into Paul, pitching both of them to the ground. Paul rolled side to side, his hands on the back of his head, groaning. He had dropped his gun.

Ethan scrambled through the dust toward the pistol.

Relic put a fresh missile into the sling and stepped into Ethan's view.

"Relic!" Ethan glanced up. "Where the hell did you come from?"

Relic looked at Ethan and Anya's eyes went from one to the other, surprised and confused. In that moment, Paul found his pistol and fired blindly toward Relic.

CHAPTER 68

Paul then spun his gun toward Ethan and Anya, forcing them to back away.

Relic released another projectile before Paul could fire at him again. The stone glanced off of Paul's right shoulder and he yelped in pain. Paul began to stand and turn, aiming at Relic more carefully this time. Relic quickly rolled over the top of the boulder behind him and disappeared.

Ethan pulled Anya towards him and they backed to the edge of the flat rock, but Paul had no interest in them for the moment. He knew where the attack had come from and was busy mounting a counter. He stood and raised his left arm to cover his head and moved quickly toward Relic's last location.

Paul strode around a corner of the cliff and felt a rock fired into his stomach. He grunted, stopped for a beat, then marched forward again. Relic turned and trotted away, leading Paul toward a jumble of huge stones that made up the landslide, away from Ethan and Anya.

Paul's head throbbed and his vision narrowed to a tunnel of light directly in front of him, but he was pissed off and powered through it. Some clown from their camp must have followed them up here. The gall of that guy, throwing stones at him! No, not throwing. He didn't know how the stones had hit him so hard. His shoulder felt like a knife was stuck in it. But he knew the guy did not have a gun and Paul was going to make him pay for his arrogance.

Paul walked cautiously around a series of car-sized boulders and saw a man scurry between a pair of high sandstone towers. He trotted confidently toward them. Where they formed a sort of entrance, he listened a moment, then darted in, swiveling from side to side. He heard boots on rock up ahead and hurried on.

Relic was running across an open plain too far for a clean shot. Paul jogged straight ahead and followed him into a junk yard of tall stones, shards of cliff fallen to the floor below, tons of burnt sandstone leaning precariously against each other.

Relic's day pack bobbed as he scrambled over the rock. Paul stopped, aimed, and fired.

CHAPTER 69

Ethan waved at Anya to join him as he followed Paul at a cautious distance. Paul was making plenty of noise, cursing and thumping awkwardly along. They ran to keep up, stopping and peering over brush and stone before each leap forward.

Ethan's heart jumped a beat when he heard another pistol shot. They hurried to the edge of a clearing where they saw Paul on the other side, staring into a dark jumble of fallen stone. He seemed uncertain for a moment then began a steady walk into the black of the tall landslide.

"You should go help the others, get them out of here," Ethan said.

"No way. I'm going to help you take this bastard out."

"But the group can get away now."

"No, they can't yet. He shot each of our rafts."

Ethan thought about what she'd said. Of course.

The two shots fired earlier, down at the camp. Thank god he'd not shot anyone there.

"OK. Time to scoot across this open area and come in behind him. If you see a good weapon anywhere, let me know," Ethan readied himself. "But at least up close we'll have a chance."

Anya pulled a folding knife from her pants pocket and locked it open. "I at least have this."

"I guess I'm still in the stone age."

She began trotting out across the open flats.

"Hey, wait for me," he said, running right behind her.

CHAPTER 70

The bullet had grazed Relic's right shoulder; he felt the wet on his shirt and smelled blood. He stumbled forward, weaving his way between the fallen stones to a cave of sorts, to a room with a high ceiling. Shafts of light fell on one side so he instinctively moved to the other. He took off his pack and laid it aside. He put another small stone in his sling, but wasn't sure he could pull it back to shoot. Along with his rifle, he had a Colt at his main camp but it was heavy, especially carried over long distances in extreme conditions. But he sure wished he had it now. Next time, he thought. If he had a next time. He scooted his back against a far, dark wall and waited.

He could hear Paul stumbling around, cursing nervously. If Relic could work his way behind the man… but the gunshot wound had drained his energy. Maybe Paul would not find him and decide he'd escaped but for now, Relic could only wait.

****

Paul seemed to find a blind alley of sorts. He back-tracked to a sharp edged monolith and tried another approach. In minutes, he reached the cave-like enclosure and peered cautiously inside. He must have sensed Relic's presence and stepped to a dark corner. They waited in silence, each hearing the other's labored breathing.

"You're hurt," Paul said. "Or you'd be throwing rocks or something at me."

Relic did not speak.

Paul felt his way slowly along a dark wall, shuffling his feet to keep from tripping over loose stones.

Relic's arm had begun to throb.

"I see you now, in front of me, sitting by the wall." His eyes had adjusted to the dark.

Relic grunted.

"You… You must be Tim," Paul said, moving closer to Relic. "I'm gonna put three slugs in your forehead, one for Harold, one for Trevor, and one for Bobby, but I want some answers first. You tell me what I want, I won't kick the shit out of you before I shoot you. I can kick a man's balls into his stomach. I've done exactly that. You can go in pain, over a long, long time, or quick and easy."

Relic remained still.

Paul relaxed his arm, letting the gun point toward the ground. He seemed to be thinking for a moment. "You are Tim, aren't you?"

Relic said nothing.

"You actually did me a big favor there, Tim. Shooting those three guys gets me way closer to big, fat Bossman. Yeah, I'll be his lead guy now, his right hand man." Paul took a step closer to Relic. "Then I'm gonna replace that fool completely. I'm after that sonofabitch and I'll have him too."

"You're a looter, a plague on this country," Relic said.

"Hell, I grew up in this country." Paul's voice was angry. "Me and my brother found shit everywhere, right on top of the ground. Arrowheads, knives, pottery. Nobody stopped us and nobody complained. Started collecting and selling when I was twelve."

"It doesn't belong to you."

"Finder's keepers."

"Bull shit."

"Enough of this." Paul took two more cautious steps toward Relic. "What the hell did you find in Horse Canyon?"

CHAPTER 71

Ethan reached the cave-like area and listened as Paul shouted at Relic. Anya appeared ahead of him, a few feet away.

Ethan motioned for her to keep working her way through the rubble to the other side of the high-ceilinged shelter. He mouthed the words, "Distract him." She nodded and climbed over a large rock and out of sight.

Shit, Ethan realized, she has the knife.

Ethan moved to the edge of the open space as quietly as he could and peered deeper into it. Paul braced himself a few feet from Relic - they could see each other easily now.

"You're going to tell me what you know about the relics in Horse Canyon..."

"Only one relic," Relic said with a smile. Exhaustion must be making him lightheaded, Ethan thought.

"Where?"

"Gone now," he chuckled.

"Shit-head. What's so special about Horse Canyon?"

"Perfect place for an ambush."

"What?"

"I'm the last person on this earth to ever tell you."

"No, you're going to be the first one to tell me." Paul lined his back leg with his front, like the punter on a football team.

Ethan moved just inside the covered area, crouching as he went. About twenty feet ahead of him was Paul's silhouette. Ethan could see Paul's back, his arms down, the pistol in his right hand.

"What the hell am I doing?" he thought. He and Anya could have gone back to the others. They could have found some way to escape, get themselves all to safety. Something was making him crazy, untethered, unafraid of the future, willing to do what he could to save a man he'd just met, yet, someone he knew better than his very best friends. He felt a strange sensation, a deep tingling, like the last of his energy, the last of his adrenaline, was bleeding away. His legs were cramping up. Anya had better hurry.

Just then, from high atop a hidden pillar, Anya dropped four stones into the chamber above Paul and

Relic, the rocks clacking down the angled shafts of sandstone to random spots on the dusty floor. Paul turned quickly and looked up, then side to side, raising his pistol.

Ethan powered forward with his legs, a sprinter off the starting block, colliding hard into Paul's back, tackling him to the ground. The gun slid from Paul's grip, skidding across the sand and Ethan reached his arm across Paul's neck and squeezed as tightly as he could.

Paul was strong, but his long arms had lost their leverage. His legs kicked and twisted and his hands slapped frantically into Ethan's head and face, but Ethan kept his weight centered on Paul's back, ignoring the stings and gouges. He knew everything depended on it.

In moments, it was clear that Ethan had control. Paul's struggles reduced quickly to futile efforts. Ethan held tight until Paul's muscles unclenched and his body collapsed in the dirt.

"Hold him, another thirty seconds," Relic said. Ethan obeyed instinctively, counting slowly in his head.

"That's enough," Relic said, touching Ethan's arm. "Don't kill him."

"Hey, down there," Anya said.

"Hey, we're OK," Ethan answered. "Come on over here." He pulled his arm from under Paul's head.

"I owe you…" Relic said to Ethan, grasping

his shoulder.

"Not half as much as I…"

Anya clamored over and around the large stones and into the high chamber.

"Nice timing," Ethan said.

"You're not so bad yourself," Anya replied, looking him up and down. She put her hands on her hips and took a deep breath. "Now what?"

CHAPTER 72

Relic sat back on his knees. "First, Ethan, stay where you are. Keep sitting on this bastard for a few minutes."

Ethan nodded.

"Pick up that pistol," he pointed, "by the barrel, and hide it somewhere in the rocks."

Anya lifted the gun like it was infected with plague and walked out of the sheltered area, back into the sunlight, and out among the jumble of scree.

Relic used his left hand to unzip his pack and reached inside. He pulled out a sturdy nylon twine and tossed it to Ethan. "Time to rope this guy up."

Ethan wrapped the twine around Paul's wrists and tied them tight. Relic pulled a small pen-knife from his pack and cut the excess string.

"Now, his feet."

Ethan repeated the process, tying Paul's feet as

closely together as he could.

"Now, put a double layer of twine around his waist, then bend his knees. Run it between his legs and tight through the twine on his feet. He won't be standing up anytime soon."

Ethan followed Relic's instructions.

Anya came back into the dark shelter. "He'll never find it," she said.

"Search him, Ethan. Make sure he doesn't have another weapon or a knife on him." Ethan went carefully through Paul's pockets. He found ammunition wrapped in an oiled cloth, two short pen-knives, cash, and a folded piece of leather.

"Look at this, will you," Ethan said, holding open the park ranger badge. "This actually looks pretty real," he said, rubbing his fingers across the raised letters.

"Toss the ammo and knives into my pack. Take the fake I.D. with you," he said to Ethan. "Hey, grab that small water bottle attached to his belt." Relic refilled it with water from his own bottle and set it close to Paul.

"Can we get the hell out of here, now?" Anya asked, sliding her way toward the exit.

CHAPTER 73

They hustled themselves out of the dark enclosure and followed Anya through the rubble and out across the open flat. When they reached the twin shafts of high sandstone, Relic found a low flat rock and sat down. Ethan and Anya stood in the sand across from him.

Relic dropped his pack to the ground and tried to examine his shoulder.

"You've been hurt," Anya said. "Let me take a look." She pulled back Relic's shirt, exposing a long, shallow cut across his shoulder blade.

"How did this happen?"

"When he shot at me. Lucky it only skimmed the top of the flesh," Relic grimaced.

"Let's get you to the boats. I've got a full med kit there."

"Hang on there a minute." Relic pulled his shirt

back on and motioned for her to step back. "We need to have a talk."

Relic pointed at Ethan. "Him I know. You, young lady, I've never actually met."

"Meet Anya," Ethan smiled broadly.

She nodded.

Relic pulled a baseball cap from his pack and put it down low on his forehead. He tucked his ponytail into the back collar of his shirt.

"How the hell did you get here?" Ethan waved toward the canyon walls.

"The river flows in a big bulge, out that way," he motioned west. "On the river, it's a dozen miles or more from Horse Canyon to here. But across the plateau, it's only a couple of miles, as the crow flies."

"But how did you know to come?"

"I stayed and watched their dig site. I figured somebody would come sooner or later, checking on their 'investment.' Sure enough... And when he hurried back into his kayak, I knew he planned to catch up with you all."

"The whole police officer thing threw me for a loop. I didn't trust him, but I didn't know what to do about it," Anya crossed her arms.

"Sure as shit, you can bet that was his plan," Relic

raised a finger. "Keep you in check."

Anya and Ethan looked at each other.

"Tell Anya what you do out here…" Ethan said.

Relic patted the air with his palms. "Stop right there. You owe me a favor, that's for sure, so here's how it's gotta be. You, young lady, owe me too. Right?"

"Yes. Right." Anya nodded earnestly.

"We all owe each other but, here's the deal. This is how it needs to be." He stopped and took a long drink of water, then a deep breath. Anya glanced nervously at the pile of giant rocks that held Paul.

"I'm just a rancher out checking for cows that wandered up the river from below. Damn things keep getting loose. I have to run my ass all over this country to find them. I was sitting here, resting, minding my own business, when who comes along but you two and some nutcase with a pistol, aiming to shoot you. I used a sling shot to help even things out. Only seemed fair." He grinned. "My name is not Relic by the way. You came up to me and thanked me and asked me directions to the closest 7-Eleven for some ice cold beer."

Ethan's eyes glimmered. A sense of confusion flickered across Anya's smile.

"I wouldn't tell you my name. I said the hell with that, I want nothing else to do with the trouble you two

seem to be in. Good or bad it means investigations, re-
ports, interviews, endless bullshit paperwork. I turned
and walked away, and there was nothing you could do
about it."

Ethan nodded.

"Clear?" Relic looked at Anya.

"Yes." She straightened. "Got it. Rancher out
looking for his cows, wandering around, probably
lost…" she said.

"With a sling shot?" Ethan asked.

"I practice with it all the time. Gotta have something if you come up on a rattler. At close range, a sling
shot can be deadly. Helped you take down that bastard,
didn't it?"

"Really?"

"Well, my rifle's back at the truck or I'd have shot
the bastard dead. Guess he's lucky that way. That much is
God's honest truth."

"Better…" Ethan nodded reluctantly.

Relic stroked his goatee. "Good. Now that that's
settled, there's something else you should know."

Anya glanced at Ethan.

Relic's dark eyes narrowed. "That jackass back
there tied up in the dirt has been sneaking around these
canyons for a couple of years now, marking up maps and

taking pictures. He's no good. Hangs with a guy they call Boss, helping him run drugs and dig up bowls and horn spoons and chert knives, and anything else that belonged to a lot of my relatives."

Ethan thought about it for a moment. "And Tim was their competition."

"This is all about these thieves. They're killing each other over a batch of old relics. They think they've hit the mother lode, but, really, Horse Canyon's all petered out."

Ethan smiled. "So, there's just nothing of any interest there, right?" He thought of the gold button he'd found in the sand. "Just maybe some worthless old relic?"

"Exactly the way the rest of the world should see it," Relic grinned.

CHAPTER 74

"Help me out a minute, would you?" Relic looked at Anya. "I've got gauze and peroxide and first aid gel in my pack."

Anya dug through the contents and pulled them out. Relic peeled his shirt from his back and leaned forward.

"This is going to sting like hell." She dabbed the wound with gauze, to wipe it clean, then poured per-oxide all over his shoulder. Relic tensed but made no sound. The liquid bubbled and mixed with his blood. Anya poured more until most of the bubbles washed away. Relic sat straight for a moment and let his skin dry. Anya found adhesive tape in Relic's pack, smeared the first aid cream onto a clean patch of gauze and laid it carefully over the wound.

"Are you sure you don't need anything from our

emergency kit, down by the boats?" She finished taping the wound and put the gauze and gear back into his pack.

"You could leave me some more peroxide, cream and bandages," Relic said. "To replace what I just used."

"Of course. Should I bring them up to you?"

"No, leave them by the boats when you go, out on the beach. I'll go down later and get 'em. Now it's time to catch me some goddamned cows..." Relic checked and closed his pack. He grabbed his shirt in his right hand, his pack in his left, and stood.

Ethan and Anya moved aside.

"*Buenos dias*," Relic saluted then turned and cut across the open flats toward a tall pile of scree below the towering cliffs.

"You can get out of here by going that way?" Anya asked Ethan, pointing toward the sheer cliffs.

"He's just going to wait for us over there, well away from the group. Then he'll get the first aid stuff from the beach."

"Oh, yes."

"But if anybody can climb over those walls, he can."

They watched as Relic wound his way between the rocks and quickly out of sight.

CHAPTER 75

They were greeted at camp with expressions of alarm and relief from the others. Ethan explained that a rancher had come upon them and helped them overcome Paul and tie him up. They'd left him tied up, but with water to drink. Later, they'd tell the authorities where to find him.

Anya and Norma cut and glued patches to the holes in both rafts. Lisa inspected and approved the results when they were done then pumped air into them until her arms ached.

It seemed to Ethan that something had changed between Millie and Darren. Millie winked at her husband and waved him closer. They smiled in earnest at each other and, together, they started to clean and pack the kitchen set-up, like they'd seen Norma do. Somehow, they'd gotten back on track.

It was noon by the time their gear was fully packed

into the rafts. Ethan felt the patches with his fingers and listened for the sound of escaping air. They seemed to work well enough, holding to the curve of inflated rubber.

"Grab some peanuts or other snacks and get on board," Anya patted her raft.

"What about this guy's kayak?" Ethan pointed. "Why don't I tie it onto my raft?"

"Great idea," Anya raised a thumb in the air. Ethan searched inside the slender kayak but didn't see anything noteworthy. He decided to leave the contents alone, for the real police to check then walked the kayak over to the raft and tied it on.

"How long will we be on the water?" Ethan asked Anya.

"We're only about four hours from the take-out spot. We're a full day late. My guess is, most of our crew from the guide shop will be down there, looking for us, or, hopefully, waiting for us."

Anya and Ethan each looked over their rafts one more time, nodded at each other, and rowed away from shore. Anya didn't ask Ethan if he was ready for a second try on the river, and he appreciated it.

In moments, they spun into the moving current and were carried away.

CHAPTER 76

Ethan let Anya's raft gain some distance from his. He pulled on the oars at a measured pace, neither hurried nor slow. A light blue sky watched them from above, clear except for a high bank of clouds miles away to the south. The sun had passed its zenith and the air was hot.

Ethan pulled the oars again as he reached the middle of the wide river. Anya was about four hundred yards ahead, rowing downstream. No doubt she wanted to get the group to safety as quickly as she could.

He listened for the tell-tale sound of whitewater, but heard none. Maybe they were through the worst of it. He dipped his right oar into the water and pulled until the raft spun around and his back faced downriver then put his strength into it, hoping to close the distance between him and the others.

A pair of crows soared across hazel-colored sandstone along the top of the canyon rim, tossing their shadows with unnatural speed and direction. They signaled some intent to each other with short, guttural caws. What they must think of us humans down here, he thought, bound by gravity to these bulbous rubber rafts, bobbing at the whim of this powerful river. Then he thought of Relic, who also might be watching them.

Ethan stopped rowing and lifted the ends of the oars into the boat. He turned to his back and looked downriver. For all his effort, Anya seemed to be pulling slowly farther away. He sighed and swung his gaze from one river bank to the other. The canyon had opened wide in this area. The chiseled walls of sandstone seemed lower now, less imposing. Acres of sandy ground, dotted with sage brush and clumps of grass, separated the water from the distant canyon walls.

The heat bore down on him, hardly a breeze to help. He opened one of the water bottles and drank deeply.

CHAPTER 77

Back in the rock fall, Paul sucked in a deep breath of air and coughed it out like an engine backfiring. He shut his eyes and shook his head, then looked blankly at his wrists. He rolled over and sat up, struggling against the twine.

"Hey!" he shouted into the shadowed chamber. "Heyyyyy…" he screamed at no one, and everyone.

****

Relic finished restocking his pack with first aid gear the rafters had left for him. Anya had added a stack of granola bars, dried fruit, brownies, and a third of a bottle of whiskey, too. God bless her.

He walked back through the box elder trees above the sandy beach to a sage-dotted flat and then to a short rise that led upriver.

Then he heard an eerie, plaintive echo radiate from the rock fall. "Shit fire," he said, as if speaking to Paul. "No need to get all pissed off about it." He grinned. "I'll be out of here quick as spit. Get back up on the rim and cut across downriver a ways. Keep this shoulder loosened up."

He adjusted his pack and made his way past a hackberry bush toward a high cone of scree at the base of the cliffs.

CHAPTER 78

Anya had stopped rowing and eventually Ethan caught up with them. Norma and Carter pulled Ethan's raft close to theirs and together they rode gentle waves into a stretch of canyon where the walls once again closed in tightly around them. The rims on either side towered high and out of sight. Blue sky narrowed into a river of its own, made of sunshine and outer space, far above them, twisting like a mirror image of the water below. A single falcon circled above. Time floated with the river.

Norma and Millie spoke a few words to each other. Carter ate peanuts and drank a can of soda. Ethan hardly heard them, listening instead to the rhythmic slap of water on the bottom of the rubber raft. A blue heron flew with them downstream.

The sound of a distant airplane interrupted the lull. The noise grew louder until a small Cessna appeared above the cliffs, its engine whining.

They watched it spiral above them. "Where are we, now?" Carter asked.

"Very close. The pick-up spot is just ahead, on river-right, about a half mile," Anya said.

"Really?" Ethan heard some disappointment in his voice.

Burnished canyon walls began to retreat from the water's edge, allowing thickets of coyote willow to root in the sandy soil. Flats spread downstream, filled with sage brush and Indian wheat. Suddenly, around the bend, tall cottonwoods lorded over a well-used beach split down the middle by a dirt and gravel two-track road. There, a little above the flat beach, sheriff's vehicles blocked the access, their red and blue strobes spinning.

Norma and Carter released Ethan's raft and when he had enough separation, he put his oars into the water and rowed onto a rocky spot on the shore. He lifted the oars back into the boat, put his hands on his knees and waited.

Anya came ashore several yards farther downstream. A pair of deputies moved slowly toward her raft, hands on their side arms. He could hear rapid questions from the officers and Anya's measured explanations. One of the deputies stared at him like the officer expected him to spontaneously combust.

The deputy finally blinked, glanced at the ground, and walked over to him. "Let me see your hands," he said.

Ethan raised them.

"What's your name?" The deputy was under six feet tall but all muscle and business. A patch on the tan baseball cap he wore announced him as a Cottonwood County Sheriff Deputy.

Ethan gave him his name.

"Step out of the raft carefully and onto the shore," the deputy directed. "Stan, get over here," he said to the other officer.

Ethan slid off the side of the boat, keeping his hands where they could be seen. His knees felt like rubber and he nearly fell to the ground. He slowly stood up, hands raised again. The deputy moved quickly and patted his back and legs, then stepped back and relaxed.

"Put your hands down. Let's get you over into the shade. Stan, get the paras in here." Stan barked something into his radio.

CHAPTER 79

An hour later, exhausted again from telling his tale to the deputy, Ethan lay back on the sand and closed his eyes. He could hear motion and voices and urgent energy all around him. Once in a while, he could hear Anya's voice among the random noise.

"Ethan," the deputy stood above him, his arm outstretched. Ethan blinked and let the officer help pull him up.

"We're about done here for now." One of the sheriff's jeeps was gone. A blue Ford van with a faded yellow River Runners sign had parked at the bottom of the road. Behind it was a trailer carrying both of the white water rafts, strapped into place. He could see the makeshift patches on both boats, covering the holes Paul had shot through them.

"Hey," Anya's voice came up from behind him.

"Hey," he turned toward her and smiled.

She glanced at her feet then back up at him. "Helluva day," she said softly.

Ethan snorted. "Helluva week," he said.

She smiled broadly at him, white teeth shining against her sun-darkened cheeks.

"You going back in the van?" he asked.

"Yeah. I assume you need a lift back into town?"

"Yeah, I guess I do."

She looked to her feet again. "What's next for you?" she asked.

"Hell if I know." He gazed off down the river, below the spot where they stood. Shades of deepened rose and hickory glowed across the chiseled sandstone. Buttes climbed on the horizon, faded and distant. His feet felt rooted in the warm sand, unable and unwilling to move.

"I've lost my wallet," Ethan shuffled his feet. "I owe the bike rental a few hundred bucks for a new bike. I'm sure by now the hotel has tossed my junk into the trash. All I have is a water bottle, borrowed from you," he, looked about, "which I seem to have lost."

"It's gotta be in the van," she pointed. "And, hey..." she looked to the ground again. He waited for her to continue.

"I've got some extra space at my place, if you need

somewhere to stay for a couple of days."

His heart fell to his stomach. "Thank you, yes, thank you," he managed to say.

"Well, then, we best get to the van," she took a step toward the rig. "Everyone's waiting for us and it's a bit of a drive back to town."

Ethan took a clear, deep breath, tired but no longer sick with exhaustion. He watched her stroll back toward the vehicle, her dark pony tail bobbing as she went, her hips swaying with the curves in the road. Her hand went behind her back, beckoning him playfully to come along. Did she just do that?

Maybe Relic is right, and we are all spirits, having a human experience. And maybe this experience isn't going to be so bad, after all.

****

In the distance, a bright line of tangerine lay on the cliffs above the river, a hint of sunset on its way. Relic tugged on his buffalo-hair beard, laid the binoculars back against his chest and smiled.

AUTHOR'S NOTE AND ACKNOWLEDGEMENTS

Thank you for reading *Desert Guardian* – I really hope you enjoyed it! As an author, I depend heavily on book reviews and referrals. So if you think others might enjoy the novel, too, please leave a quick review on Amazon and on any other internet site you use for selecting books to read. *The moment it takes to leave a quick rating makes a lasting difference for the author!*

Someone once said that a creative work is never really finished – just abandoned. The trick, of course, is knowing *when* to abandon it. I hope I am leaving this one at the curb at roughly the right time.

I thank Dad for teaching me to canoe, Mom for teaching me to write, and both for their endless encouragement. Mom, the very first copy of this is yours.

Thanks to my incredible wife Gina and my family for letting me disappear for hours and days at a time while working on this effort and for their valued comments and contributions. I could not have written or abandoned it without them.

Thanks also to Gina, Sarah, Adam, Sarajean, Nate and my friends who have shared canoes and rafts with me over the decades -- Doug, Dave, Ron, Jeff, Bridger, and many others. The rivers of this nation deserve and depend on our respect and preservation. Their waters are sacred.

I thank Jim Dempsey, Associate Editor at Novel Gazing, for his careful attention to detail and insightful suggestions. And I thank Nate again for the incredible map and chapter art.

Thanks to Daniel Thiede for the fabulous cover art and text layout.

And, finally, I thank the many people who have inspired the characters in this work.

The tent became a dome of light, then began to smolder and burst into flame near the back, near the kitchen stove.

"Hey, we just cleaned the grill back there," Relic said, making Wyatt laugh.

The fire spread slowly, casting a halo of light across the camp. Security guards hollered, workers yelled their curses and questions, and everyone rushed to see what the commotion was all about.

"Is she really crazy enough to do that?" Wyatt asked.

"Yep," Relic nodded.

"Well, shee-it," Wyatt did his best imitation of Faye.

Relic smiled. "Don't let her hear you or she'll knock your block off."

"No doubt."

"Would you see what you can do to slow down that backhoe up ahead of us and anything else with a lock and key? Then work your way north, swing back toward the staircase and we can meet up there."

Wyatt nodded.

"Keep a close look out. They'll be searching as soon as the mess [kitchen tent] is under control."

"What's your next move?" Wyatt asked.

Relic jerked his thumb toward the portable toilets.

"Really?" Wyatt said.

Relic turned and faded into the dark. Wyatt heard footfalls, someone moving quickly toward him. After a moment, he recognized her shape bobbing along. She tossed something and he heard it clacking into the bed of a pickup. She nearly ran into him.

"Hey." He put his hands out toward her.

"Hey," she said, slowing, but only a bit. "Here." She tossed a stick of dynamite to him, the fuse sparkling lit.

"Shit!"

"Throw it!" she shouted as she ran past. "Now!"

Wyatt stared at the tube in his hand. The fuse sputtered and spat and shortened with every second, time compressed with the tightness of his breath, the glowing fuse moving forward immutably until something like a spinning clutch popped in his chest and muscle movement became possible again. He reached his arm back and threw it as far and as fast as he could, then he spun and ran to the side of another truck and turned back to look.

The pickup Faye had tossed something into rose into the air with a smack that washed away all other sound, then fell back to the ground with a nasty twist as pieces of sheet metal dropped from the sky.

"Holy…"

Wyatt's stick of dynamite exploded somewhere beyond another truck, lighting something on fire, sending a second sonic boom through his skull, making him jump in his tracks. He stared at the blaze as it settled into a steady burn and looked the direction Faye had run.

A third, fourth, and fifth explosion erupted in quick succession in the row of portable toilets and Wyatt knew it was Relic's work. Where was Relic's peaceful resistance now? Lord, he hoped no one was in those toilets. Then, he thought, what a mess of shit, and he giggled and smacked his hands together.

Oh, my god, was it possible to have so much fun? He never expected stopping Lord Winnieship from stealing this canyon to feel so damn good.

He stared at the fire he'd started and tried to think. He wanted to follow Faye but there was no telling what other mayhem she had in mind, and he did not want to walk into an exploding outhouse. He tried to regulate his breathing, with only a little luck. He circled away from the path Faye had taken, giving her a wide berth, moving to the outer edge of the parked vehicles.

Wyatt turned and trotted toward a lone backhoe, maybe sixty yards away. Though the electric lights of the compound were out, the kitchen and dining room blaze cast a sallow glow on the tops of the other tents and equipment. The upper arm of the yellow backhoe was lit like a candle.

His shins scraped across brittle sage and he slowed to a walk. He'd lost his own toothpicks, so that trick [of jamming the locks] would not work with the heavy equipment. After Faye's dynamite, toothpicks seemed pretty pathetic anyway. Maybe there was a set of keys kept in the ignition that he could toss away. Or maybe he could flatten its tires or pull wires from under the dash to disable the beast. He turned to watch the bobbing of flashlights all around the burning mess tent a quarter of a mile away. The voices of men rose and fell in a rhythm that was almost musical, like an offbeat composition.

He stopped at the base of the backhoe and stared up at the top, where the boom and dipper attached. He circled the machine to the open cabin and peered inside.

"Stop and turn around." The voice was deep and familiar.

Wyatt turned and raised his hands. Even in the semi-dark, Lynch's muscled bulk identified him immediately. He held a pistol aimed at Wyatt's chest.

"You!" Lynch said. "You sonofabitch."

Wyatt saw the left hook a milli-second before it struck his jaw, wrenching his head away and toward the ground. He stumbled to the side. A blow to his stomach struck like a rocket and his chest ached, all the veins in his body shut down by a sonic boom. Slivers of light flashed through his eyes, closed tight against the assault. He sensed himself floating to the earth, his muscles turned to liquid. He was out before he hit the dirt.

WINGS OVER GHOST CREEK

Owen thought his heart had completely halted, and it had, for just a second, and then it began a pounding, deep and strained, pumping blood through his temple in spurts then galloping quickly, flushing his cheeks.

Holy flying eff.

He sucked a shallow breath of air, pulled his gaze from the dead arm, and looked back the way he'd come. From this perspective, the arm was well-hidden on the backside of the long pile of dirt, tucked close to the low rock face and well out of view from the hangar and the tents beyond. Last night's heavy storm had flushed loose soil from the canyon slopes and probably from the body, too. He tried not to look back at the fragile hand, but he couldn't help himself. Skin shriveled against the tiny bones, stiff leather holding the assembly of joints together, keeping the fingers pointed in confusing, haphazard directions, their owner not sure which way to go. Red nail polish added a cheap party flare, a celebration completely out of place.

Holy eff. Hold it together, he told himself, get back to camp and pretend he'd never seen it. Tell Thomas. No one else. Someone here could have killed this girl, must have killed her. Why? What had happened here?

He turned his eyes to his feet and shuffled across the ground, moving to the edge of the pile of dirt. He peered around the mound and saw the edge of the hangar and the back of the tents. No one seemed to be around, so he hustled away from the dirt, across the hard-packed surface, and into the hangar. He went to the yellow plane again and leaned on the right strut, his breath still shallow and labored.

Owen looked beyond the hangar to the field outside and the Cessna waiting for them. Where was Thomas?

"Did you get that cold drink?"

Panic charged through his brain, a devil's hot wire crackling from one ear to the other. His head jerked toward the front of the plane and he clamped his hands tightly on the strut. Everett's question was smooth but – was there an undertone in his voice?

Owen managed to force a breath.

"No…" he patted the wing support, glanced at Everett, then spoke to the plane itself, too nervous to look at the man again. Squeezing the strut helped him to focus. "I got sidetracked by this old Aeronca. What year is it, do you know?"

"1946, I'm told."

"Oh."

"Are you a pilot?" Everett moved out of the sunlight and into the shade of the hangar. Owen knew the man could see him better now.

"No, no, I'm not. Tried to take some lessons, but…" He struggled to keep his thoughts on the aircraft, away from what he'd discovered. "Just look at this panel, the instrument panel," he pointed. "Not hardly any instruments here, though. It's all metal, too, like the dashboards on old cars." He kept his eyes on the cockpit, still reluctant to look directly at Everett.

"Yeah, I've looked it over myself." Everett's voice seemed more normal now, more conversational. "The owner has a friend who came out here a couple of days ago. He's restoring the old bird, but I don't know how far he's gotten. The fabric looks like a stiff breeze would pull it off." He ran his hand across the edge of the wing opposite Owen. "You wouldn't catch me flying in this death trap." Everett wandered away from the plane, plucked a long blade of grass from the ground and began to twist it absentmindedly.

"Yeah, the cloth on this one needs completely replaced." Owen tried to sound like an authority on the subject and felt his nerves calm a little as he spoke. He ducked under the wing and walked into the sunlight.

"Seen my boss?"

"I think he's about done," Everett pointed toward the tents along Ghost Creek. Thomas and Angela were walking slowly back toward the Cessna. Angela was explaining something, Thomas nodding.

"Well, it was nice meeting you." Everett moved quickly toward Owen and offered his hand, his smile show-room friendly, his shake cold and curt.

"Yes. Nice meeting you, too." Owen made eye contact briefly and turned back toward the Cessna. "Better get going."

He strode toward the rented Park Service plane, muscle memory moving his legs, thoughts flowing back to that tortured hand, its ragged movement in the breeze. He tried to be nonchalant about getting the hell out of there. Angela and Thomas came closer to the Cessna.

"Got what we need?" Owen asked Thomas.

Thomas looked up. "Yep. Thanks for the tour and good luck to you," he said to Angela. He shook hands with her and Everett and turned back to the plane.

Owen did not wait to be told to climb in. He adjusted his seatbelt, put the headset on, and waited. Thomas did the same.

How was he going to tell Thomas about the dead girl's arm? When should he tell him? Angela and Everett positioned themselves to one side and in front of the Cessna. They could see any conversation between him and Thomas, so he stayed quiet.

Thomas spent a moment examining the air map and checking the instruments. Out of the corner of his eye, Owen saw the man with the red hat, Luke, run up to Everett and whisper urgently in his ear. Everett glared at the plane, then gave some sort of order to Luke, who ran out of view. Did they know he'd found the girl's body?

"Clear prop!" Thomas pumped the throttle and turned the key, the engine spitting to life. Owen sat back in his seat, eyes straight ahead, and listened to the engine as Thomas adjusted the fuel mixture and checked the magnetos, turning first one off, then the other, then both back on for flight, Owen wishing he would hurry the hell up. Thomas finally pushed the throttle forward and the engine roared, the Cessna shuddered, and they began to roll down the dirt strip, vibrating, bouncing, jarring over small ruts until suddenly, liftoff, and the ride became smooth and even, the engine solid and throaty, clear air ahead of them, and Owen finally took a deep breath.

Thomas made a gentle turn to their left, flying back toward the creek, the dig site, and the old hangar, circling to gain altitude needed to fly over the plateau above the camp. They rose steadily as they went, Owen thinking how to explain what he'd found, hoping he'd done the right thing by waiting until they were in the air, bound for home base.

They leveled out about two miles past the Quonset hut, aiming for the broad Colorado River as they continued to climb beyond the canyon. A ribbon of dust rose to their right, a truck in motion along the road, soon to be well behind them. Ghost Creek faded from view as they neared the level of the plateau. They could see the bronze river beyond as it wound its way southward, on toward the Grand Canyon, on to the Gulf of California. Owen rubbed his hands on his pants and readied himself.

"Thomas," he spoke into the microphone on his headset.

"Yes?"

"I've got something to tell you, something I discovered down there while you were with the archeologist..."

"Yes?" Thomas checked his GPS and adjusted his heading.

Just then, a hollow thump jarred Thomas forward and he pushed the yoke in, then tugged and released it as he slumped back in his seat. Owen grabbed the yoke and his eyes swelled wide and he stared at Thomas' slackened face and began to scream his name, bobbing the plane's nose up, down, up, when another hollow thump jarred them and oil sprayed into the air and onto the right side of the windshield and he heard the motor cough, and cough again, and felt the Cessna lose its power, dropping in the air, descending toward the ground and he screamed again.

DIAMONDS OF DEVIL'S TAIL

"Wicked chickens lay deviled eggs, but this one's rotten, too." Relic took the binoculars from his eyes and stroked his buffalo-beard goatee. Something about the man on the trail below made his skin tingle.

He slid away from the edge, out of the man's line of sight, and looked about. An unlikely descendant from clans of the Hopi and Scottish, Relic wandered the remote reaches of the Green and Colorado Rivers and the high plateaus between them, a weathered hermit at home in the desert outback, roaming ancient trails, brewing his homemade gin at a couple of narrow, spring-fed crags tucked above the floodplains. He tightened his ponytail, errant strands of white flashing through his coal-black hair.

A dried-out branch of cottonwood leaned against the nearest in a row of six Pueblo houses nestled tightly between the floor and ceiling of the cliff, a string of separate rooms, their stone blocks still mortared together in the corners. Inside were mano stones, held in the hand for grinding corn, and metate, wide-bottom slabs used for the same purpose. A child's bow and arrow, chert for making knives and arrowheads, and bowls of corn, squash, and other seeds were set neatly on indoor ledges under a layer of dust; their owners, it seemed, only away for the winter. In the farthest room were a row of large pots painted with white and black bolts of lightning, edges curved and sharp, with handles on their sides, tops still sealed tight, their contents a thousand year-old mystery. Relic meant to keep it that way.

He leaned forward again. The man strode purposefully toward the high cliff with something long, something strangely out of place, glinting in the desert sun. He put the binoculars back to his eyes.

Of all the things to be lugging in this remote country, to be balancing on bony shoulders in the noonday heat, that angular, outrageous shape was an aluminum ladder, designed for the suburban handyman.

"Well, shit on a shingle." Relic tucked the binoculars away, lay flat near the ruins, and waited.

The man struggled awkwardly up the trail, finally dragging the extension ladder to a stop at the base of the sandstone cliff. He wiped the sweat from his forehead and gazed upward at the solid, sloping rock and the extreme measures the Pueblo people had taken to keep their houses and granaries hidden and safe, high in the cliffs and crags, deep in the desert outback. Centuries ago, they carried masonry, mortar, and jars of water up rickety, wooden ladders to build these solid structures; hard, hot work with just one purpose – protection against interlopers. Now the man below had a ladder of his own, and he rested it against the stone and tugged on the rope that extended it upward, the arms squealing in their tracks, each rung clunking into place as it went.

The man shifted an empty duffle bag across his shoulders and began climbing carefully, one step at a time.

The twenty-eight foot ladder shifted suddenly an inch to the side, but it seemed to find a new, more solid base. The man flexed his knees, testing to make sure the aluminum would not slide any farther, and glanced up. The top of the ladder reached just above the lip of the sandstone ledge.

That man must think he'll find a load of artifacts up here, Relic thought, maybe even lower them to the ground by rope from the ruins, then step back down the ladder unencumbered. But the ancient Pueblo had one last line of defense.

Relic rolled away from the ruins and shifted along the ledge until he was directly in front of the top rung of the ladder, waiting. He listened as the man placed one hand on the step above him, then the next, one at a time, rising cautiously higher.

The man reached the cap of the ledge, but when he looked across the level shelf, where the stone walls rested, there, alone in the red dust, sat Relic looking, he knew, like a weathered Pueblo man, a ghost of the ruins, with a black goatee and a pony tail, holding a three foot cottonwood branch as thick as his arm.

"Shit!" the man's foot slid off one rung and down to the next. "Holy mother…who the hell are you?"

Relic's dark eyes squinted, his lips rose at the corners, and he slid the branch toward the man's ladder.

"What the hell?" the man tightened his grip.

Relic placed the branch on the top rung and began to push.

"No! Shit, no!" He raised his hand for a flash then returned it to the ladder. "You'll kill me!"

Relic slowly pushed the ladder away from the ledge, forcing it to twist outward on one end, then the other, as it lifted from the face of the cliff.

The man dropped both feet to the lower rung and slid his hands quickly down the aluminum sides, dropping his feet, holding for a moment, dropping, holding, dropping as the ladder leaned farther and farther away from the cliff, more and more upright above, ready to catapult him into a pile of rocks, and just as his feet hit the dirt the ladder tipped past its balance, dipped over-

head and spun out of his hands and onto the rocky
ground with a *clang,* a bounce, and another *clang!*

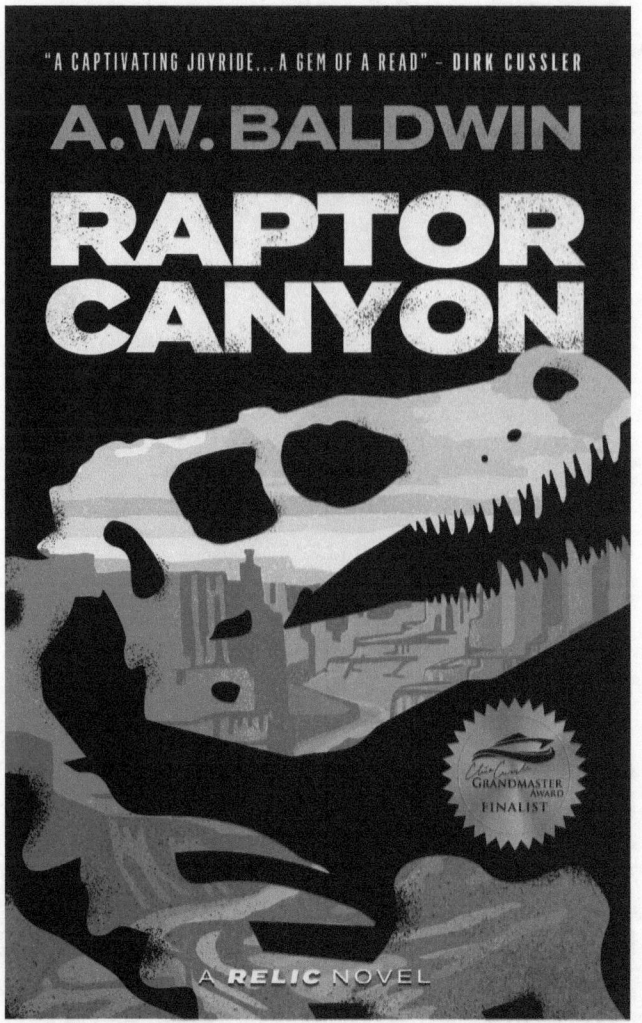

What if you discover you've helped your boss hide a murder and defile a pristine canyon? Can a young lawyer and moonshining hermit save rare petroglyphs and monkey-wrench a corrupt land deal in the Utah canyons?

An impromptu murder leads a hermit named Relic to an unlikely set of dinosaur petroglyphs and swindlers using the unique rock art to turn a pristine canyon into a high-end tourist trap. When attorney, Wyatt, and his boss travel to the site to approve the next phase of financing, Wyatt learns the truth about their unorthodox role in the project. A corrupt security chief runs Relic and Wyatt off of the site and the unusual pair must endure each other while fleeing though white-water rapids, remote gorges, and hidden caverns. Faye, who shares covert ties with the treasured site, catalyzes their desperate plan to fight back and to recast the fate of Raptor Canyon.

Buy now from a bookstore near you or *amazon.com*

ALSO AVAILABLE FROM

A. W. BALDWIN

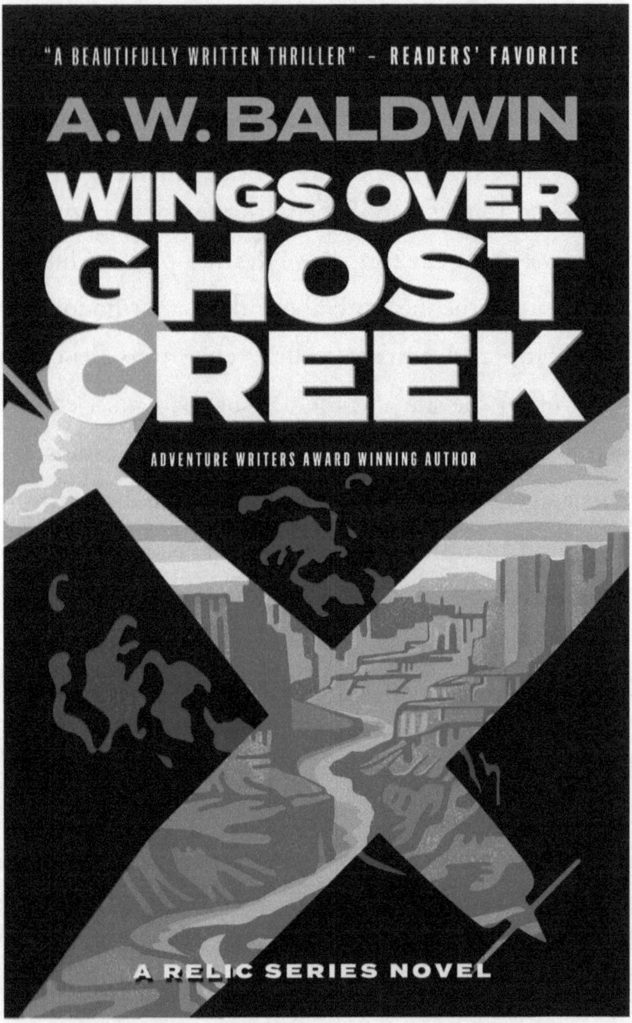

What if your archeology field class was hiding assassins and dealers in black-market treasure?

Owen discovers a murdered corpse at a college-run archeological dig in the Utah outback but when he and a park service pilot try to reach the sheriff for help, their plane is shot from the sky. Owen must ditch the aircraft in the Colorado River, where he is saved by a moonshining hermit named Relic. The two flee from the sniper and circle back to warn the students. They must trek through rugged canyon country, unravel a baffling mystery, and foil a remarkable form of thievery. Suzy, a student at the dig, helps spearhead their escape but the unique team of crooks has a surprise for them...

Buy now from a bookstore near you or *amazon.com*

When diamonds appear in a remote canyon stream, whitewater rafters and artifact thieves set off in a deadly race to the source.

Brayden, an aspiring writer, works in a Chicago insurance firm with his ambitious uncle when they embark on a wilderness whitewater adventure. On a remote hike, they find their colleague, Dylan, dead in the sand, a handful of gems in his fist. When thieves charge in, Brayden flees deeper into the canyon, where he encounters a gin-brewing recluse named Relic. Brayden's uncle is cornered and cuts a deal with the thieves, but they each have a surprise for the other… and the rafters have ideas of their own about getting rich quick… Brayden and Relic must become allies, traverse the harsh desert, and beat the thieves to the hidden gems. Brayden must confront his uncle about suspicious payments at their insurance firm and what he was really doing at the stream where Dylan was killed…

Can they discover the truth, find the lost jewels, and protect the rafters from grenade-tossing thieves?

Buy now from a bookstore near you or *amazon.com*